"Admit it, Courtney. All morning long you've felt the same thing I have," Jared said. "And you're too passionate to act like an icicle."

"Icicle! Darn you, Jared Calhoun, how's this?" She reached for him, saw the flare of surprise—or was it satisfaction—in his eyes. She locked her arms around his neck, put her lips firmly on his, and kissed for all she was worth. And he returned it, perhaps for all he was worth too. It seemed that way to Courtney because it jolted her like an explosion. She burned and trembled and responded as his lips tasted hers leisurely, becoming a pleasure that erased his accusation. It was an effort to remember that she was trying to prove a point. Finally she pulled away, and her voice emerged in a breathless whisper.

"Now will you go home?"

"Not in a million years," he said huskily. "That was the kind of kiss a man dreams about."

"Was it the kiss of an icicle?"

"I'm not sure. Let's try again and I'll give you an answer . . ."

WHAT ARE *LOVESWEPT* ROMANCES?

They are stories of true romance and touching emotion. We believe those two very important ingredients are constants in our highly sensual and very believable stories in the *LOVESWEPT* line. Our goal is to give you, the reader, stories of consistently high quality that may sometimes make you laugh, sometimes make you cry, but are always fresh and creative and contain many delightful surprises within their pages.

Most romance fans read an enormous number of books. Those they truly love, they keep. Others may be traded with friends and soon forgotten. We hope that each *LOVESWEPT* romance will be a treasure—a "keeper." We will always try to publish

LOVE STORIES YOU'LL NEVER FORGET
BY AUTHORS YOU'LL ALWAYS REMEMBER

The Editors

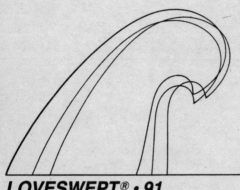

LOVESWEPT® • 91
Sara Orwig
Calhoun and Kid

BANTAM BOOKS
TORONTO • NEW YORK • LONDON • SYDNEY • AUCKLAND

CALHOUN AND KID

A Bantam Book / May 1985

LOVESWEPT® *and the wave device are registered*
trademarks of Bantam Books, Inc. Registered in U.S. Patent
and Trademark Office and elsewhere.

ISBN 0-553-21704-6

Published simultaneously in the United States and Canada

Bantam Books are published by Bantam Books, Inc. Its trademark,
consisting of the words "Bantam Books" and the portrayal of a
rooster, is Registered in U.S. Patent and Trademark Office and in
other countries. Marca Registrada. Bantam Books, Inc., 666 Fifth
Avenue, New York, New York 10103.

PRINTED IN THE UNITED STATES OF AMERICA

O   0 9 8 7 6 5 4 3 2 1

To the hero at home . . .

One

Below a gray sky a narrow gravel trail wound through a densely wooded area of oaks, red cedars, hackberries, and brown, dry underbrush. A cluster of people were standing on the trail, two men and five women, binoculars in hand as they studied a bird perched in an oak. Courtney Meade, a slender woman in a tan jacket, white knit shirt, and jeans, her golden hair plaited in one long braid that hung down her back, had pointed out a hermit thrush. She glanced at the group of birdwatchers and waited while one of them, Henry Twilling, raised his camera to snap the bird's picture.

Even as he focused on the bird, a nearby shot blasted the crisp February air, shattering the quiet and sending a flock of birds flapping from the surrounding trees. Courtney stiffened and looked at the group of bird-watchers. As Miss Barnhill paled and swayed, Henry Twilling held her arm to steady her. Another bang sent more birds skyward. When the third shot reverberated loudly, Courtney left the trail, plunging through brown grass and sumac as she raced the short distance to the eastern boundary, to the fence that separated the nature sanctuary from a horse farm.

She emerged from the trees to face a man standing by the fence. He was wearing sneakers, jeans, a sheepskin jacket, and a battered, broad-brimmed black hat. A few yards behind him stood a sorrel horse. His rifle was aimed at the sky, and he fired twice in rapid succession.

"Stop that!" Courtney called out, racing to the fence.

He lowered the gun to look at her, leveling cold blue eyes that appeared as lethal as the weapon. Momentarily startled, Courtney gazed at him. The hat was pushed to the back of his head, allowing wavy brown hair to tumble over his forehead. With languid insolence his eyes lowered in a thorough appraisal that didn't miss one inch of her five feet and six inches, from her blond hair to her sneakers. For a moment Courtney forgot her anger. His assessment was wholly masculine, startling her into self-consciousness, into a brief awareness of male and female. Then his eyes met hers again, and her anger returned.

"This is a nature sanctuary, mister," she said. "You can't shoot the birds!"

"This is a horse ranch, sister, and one of those damned birds is causing trouble! On my side of the fence."

"You're crazy!"

"The hell I am! You've got a red-tailed hawk—"

"Ebeneezer?" Courtney gasped.

"Dammit! Is that bird a pet?"

"Well, sort of . . ."

"He's going to be sort of dead if I see him fly over this fence again!"

"You can't kill him!"

"Like hell!" A strong, firm jaw covered in dark stubble jutted out in a no-nonsense fashion while white teeth clamped down on a cigar. Courtney suddenly felt her peaceful life was being threatened by this stubborn, angry neighbor.

"It's downright ornery to shoot at a bird!" she snapped, trembling with frustration, aware that the bird-watchers were beginning to emerge from the woods and listen to the confrontation—which didn't seem to matter to the man one whit.

"I'm not half as mean and ornery as that damned bird," he said.

"What has Ebeneezer done to you?"

"He's scared my horses, made them run away, and jangled their nerves." His voice lowered to a menacingly low tone. "And he's done it deliberately!"

"Oh, aren't you absurd!"

"No. If that bird could snicker, he would. And that's not all—"

Just then there was a loud squawk, a flutter of wings, and a large, speckled hawk settled on a myrtle bush on Courtney's side of the fence. The man swore and raised the gun.

"Don't you aim at him!" Courtney cried. "He's in a protected sanctuary. I have witnesses!"

"It'd be worth paying a fine and going to jail to be rid of him!" The man leveled the gun, and in spite of the fact that they were well out of range, everyone behind Courtney moved to one side.

"Now, see here!" Courtney said, but the man paid her no attention.

Desperate, wanting to save her son's pet, she jumped over the fence. The man saw her move and lowered his gun. Her foot hit the top rail, and she fell against him, knocking him down. She hit his solid middle with a jolt that sent a pain vibrating down her shoulder, through her side and hip.

The gun exploded and the man yelled, then spewed forth a stream of curses that did cause Miss Barnhill to faint.

Courtney thought she was going to faint too. Dizziness swirled over her, making her cling to hard shoulders. She was lying on top of a long, lean body, but then she was flung aside. She looked at the man and saw a red stain darkening one of his sneakers.

"Oh, my word, you're shot!"

"Yes, darling, thanks to you!"

There was a rustle of wings and Ebeneezer landed on the man's hat. The man swore, trying to grab Ebeneezer, who flapped away with an angry squawk.

"So help me, I'm going to kill him!" the man said.

Courtney truly felt faint. She had caused the man to shoot himself. Everything spun and she blinked. "I hurt you!"

"You might say so, yes."

"Can I help you home? Do you have someone to drive you to the hospital? I'm so sorry, I didn't mean to cause you any harm. I was just trying to save the hawk. He's our pet." She realized she was babbling, but she couldn't stop the stream of words.

"Stay the hell away from me, kid. Take your bird lovers and shove—"

"Don't be vulgar! Do you have someone to drive you to the hospital?"

"No, but thanks anyway. You've done enough for one day."

Courtney turned around. "Mr. Twilling, will you lead the group back? I'll see about this man."

"Of course," Mr. Twilling said, looking doubtfully at the two of them. "May I be of help, Courtney?"

"No. I'll go with him to the hospital."

"Like hell," the man said.

"Stop swearing with every breath! There are ladies present who aren't accustomed to that sort of language."

For a fleeting second she saw a flicker in his blue eyes, a slightly startled expression, but it was gone swiftly, replaced by rage. "Join your damned bird lovers and leave me alone!" he snapped.

She looked at the side of his tennis sneaker, which was becoming drenched in blood, and felt a sickening lurch in her middle because it was her fault. She couldn't bear to see someone in pain.

"Please, let's get you to a hospital," she said.

"Don't want me to bleed to death right here, eh?"

"Oh, don't talk that way. If I hold you, can you get up?"

"I can get up if you don't hold me!"

"You're so darned pesky! Get up and I'll help you to your horse!"

She thought she saw another glimpse of surprise cross his features. When his lips firmed, she wondered if he had just bitten back a laugh. Surely not; he looked too fierce for laughter.

"It's a damned good thing you're underage," he said. "They'll go easier on a female minor for assault."

"Your brain is about as active as your manners," she said. "Stand up and I'll help you to a car!" This time when he ducked his head, she felt sure he was hiding a smile.

"Florence Nightingale, you're not! Give me your arm, kid." He took hold of her arm, coming up off the ground with almost no pull whatsoever. He was lean and wiry, and towered over her. She saw him wince in pain as he shifted his weight and swore.

"I'm sorry," she said.

"Not half so much as I am. And, kid, you're going to be a hell of a lot sorrier soon."

"I'm not a kid."

His eyes narrowed, and she received another appraisal. "How old are you?"

"Goodness, you lack manners! You don't ask a wom—"

"Forget I asked. I don't feel like chatting. If you insist on helping me, we'd better get back to my house." He whistled, and the sorrel walked over to him.

"Can I go get a car and come back?" Courtney asked.

"No."

The word ended all discussion. He secured his rifle in its boot, grasped the saddle, and hoisted himself up on his stomach. Swearing the entire time, he swung his leg over the horse. When he sat up straight, his face was pale. Courtney shuddered when she saw how the ground and his foot were speckled with blood, then climbed up behind him. Once settled, she gazed in consternation at his broad shoulders. There was something about the man that made her reluctant to touch him.

"You better hold on," he said over his shoulder. "Don't be bashful."

She slipped her arms around his narrow waist, only to discover that her first inclination had been right. Contact with this man was as jolting as locking arms around a burning piece of metal. She stared at the back of his head. His dark brown wavy hair was neatly clipped and lay on a tanned neck. He smelled nice, an enticing scent that didn't fit. He looked as if he should smell like leather and dust and sweat. She wondered at that. His clothes had been neat and clean—before he was shot.

As they rode in silence her spirits were drooping, but they soon plummeted when she felt him sway in the saddle.

"Oh, my! Are you all right?"

He didn't answer as a shudder wracked him.

"Please don't faint."

"Wouldn't think of it," he said, but all the force had gone out of his words.

"Mister, is there anyone at your house, any men who work for you or your wife?"

"No one," he answered with terrifying cheer. She would have welcomed his anger.

"Guy's gone," he added.

Her spirits sank further. No help at his house. "Do you have car keys?"

"In my right pocket."

She glared at the back of his head. She wasn't about to reach into the pocket of a pair of jeans that fit slender hips like a second skin!

"Can you get them out for me?" she asked.

He chuckled and her face burned. She felt a faint twinge of anger, but fear overrode it.

"Do you have insurance?" she asked.

"What?"

"Do you have hospitalization insurance?" she yelled, praying he wouldn't faint.

"Don't yell in my ear, dammit!"

"Then answer my question!"

"What question?" He slurred the words and her heart jumped with fright.

"Do you"—she enunciated each word clearly and slowly—"have hospitalization?"

"Yeah, kid. I'm not deaf, just shot in the foot."

"Who carries your hospitalization?"

"I do."

"No. What company? Give me the name of a company or they won't admit you to the hospital."

"Jersey Standard." He laughed. "Sounds like a cow."

"Oh, dear." The man was becoming delirious; she was sure of it. "How much farther to your car?"

"About ten hours."

"Oh, no!" Courtney swayed as a rush of emotion buffeted her, and she tightened her arms around him. Reason set in quickly, though, and she realized in ten hours' time she could ride his horse to the nearest hospital and home again. "It isn't either!" she snapped. "How long until we reach your house?"

"Another minute or two."

"Don't tell me ten hours! You almost made me faint!"

When he laughed, she was convinced he was delirious. It was a nice, pleasant chuckle, incongruous with his stern features.

"Your wife's not home?"

"Don't have a wife, kid."

She could understand why not. "Who's your next of kin? If you lose consciousness . . ."

"I won't."

"You don't know!" She was wavering between fear for his injury and rage over his personality.

"I won't faint."

"Who's the next of kin?"

"Who's *your* next of kin? We may need to notify them when you go to jail."

Her heart lurched, and the full ramifications of what she had done came thundering down on her with the force of an eighteen-wheeler. "It's Ryan." She could barely say the words.

"Ryan, huh? Father, brother . . . boyfriend?"

"I'm twenty-nine years old!"

"Son-of-a-gun! I'm getting ancient when a twenty-nine-year-old looks sixteen."

His words had trailed off, and suddenly he

slumped and started to fall. She tightened her arms, pulling him back against her. "Mister!"

She felt him straighten. "It's Jared, kid."

"I'm not a kid. My name is Courtney."

"Courtney, in jeans and a long pigtail. Ever shot anyone before?"

"I didn't shoot you." Her voice was glacial. "You shot yourself."

"You caused it."

"I'm so sorry!"

"So you've said. That Ebeneezer is a goner. I mean the next time that stinking bird comes into my sights—blam!"

Courtney closed her eyes and shivered. "You're a cussed, ornery, bird-hating jerk!"

"And you, kid, are a lethal, infuriating bit of female fluff!"

Courtney shook with rage, momentarily not worrying about his foot. She drew herself up and said coldly, " 'Trust not the man who hath no love/for sparrow, jay, the wren, the dove . . .' Beaufort Elling."

" 'Beware the dame/who makes you lame'— Calhoun."

"Calhoun who?"

"Jared Calhoun."

"I should have known," she ground out through clenched teeth.

He chuckled.

"In the whole state of Tennessee, why, oh, why, did you have to buy a farm next-door to a nature sanctuary?"

"In the whole state of Tennessee, why, oh, why, do I have to live next door to an evil-hearted hawk named Ebeneezer?"

"You can move."

"Or eliminate Ebeneezer."

"That's murder."

"What you did may be murder. Shooting a tres-passing, ornery hawk isn't!"

"Mr. Calhoun, you are the most irritating, ras-cally man."

"If that's an example of your worst volley of words, kid, you need to broaden your vocabulary."

Burning with fury, she was relieved to glimpse a brown house through the trees ahead. "There's your home. Get out your car keys."

"Get them out yourself."

"Do you want me to take you to the hospital?"

"Frankly, no. Kid, I hate to break the news, but I'd just as soon never see you again until the trial."

She gritted her teeth. Could he put her in jail? Or was he teasing? "Mr. Calhoun, I'm sorry. I didn't mean to shoot you. I *didn't* shoot you—you did it! But I didn't mean to cause you to shoot your-self." She felt flustered and frightened and angry.

"Tell it to the judge. Get the keys out of my pocket."

"You're perverted."

"You're old-maidenish, a prude, a twenty-nine-year-old who must be scared of men." He reached into his pocket and held the keys over his shoul-der.

She snatched them away from him stiffly. His accusation had hurt. "Thank you. You're a first-class jerk, sir."

"So you said. I'm shot and bleeding, we hope not fatally, from a gun wound inflicted by one Courtney . . . Courtney what?"

"Courtney Meade." She could have added Mrs., but she didn't want to prolong her conversation with him. She wanted to take him to a doctor and get away from him.

"Son-of-a-gun!" he said softly, and touched her ring finger. He turned, surprise in his voice. "You're married!"

His shoulder pressed into a soft, full breast and she tried to lean back away from him. He looked amused. There was no doubt about it this time, even though his features were as solemn as an owl's. She saw the slight fanning of wrinkles from the corners of his eyes, and it softened his harsh features. It made him attractive. She swallowed.

"I'm divorced." She tried to speak with dignity.

He smiled, and it was devastating, like Mount Saint Helens erupting, changing all his features. His teeth were white and even. Creases developed in his cheeks. Laugh lines fanned from his eyes, and he became appealing. Warm, appealing, inviting . . . as if she could be coaxed to smile in return.

Which she would have been happy to do if she could have forgotten his ornery personality. The smile was a trick played by nature, a device like the pretty appeal of a Venus flytrap to lure an unsuspecting fly to be devoured. Well, she wasn't falling for his smile because she knew what was behind it: A bird-hating monster who would murder Ebeneezer if he had a chance!

She drew herself up. His gaze rested on her mouth, and it became more difficult to remain poised and cool. He had an intense way of watching her that was disturbing. Her lips tingled and she clamped them together.

His laugh lines deepened. "Son-of-a-gun," he whispered. "I would've guessed you'd never been kissed in your life."

"Oh, thanks a heap!"

"You look like a prickly pear, kid."

"I *look* like one? That's the limit, coming from a bristly burr like you!" she said acidly, burning and hating the flush that crept into her cheeks. Now she wished he would faint. "Will you turn around?"

"Curiosity has me, kid. You know . . ." He

squinted at her, and her breathing stopped. There was some silent, electric message in that squint that altered her system. She felt her anger dissipate like air out of a popped balloon. And in place of the anger came awareness. Absolute awareness of Jared Calhoun as a man and of herself as a woman. As obnoxious as he was, he was all man and she knew it, with a sudden tingle, down to the soles of her feet.

"Turn around," she whispered.

"I'll be damned," he said in a voice that was like warm springwater swirling all around her. "You are a woman."

As his gaze lowered to her breasts she blushed hotly. She couldn't control the reaction she felt. Her jacket was open and he could clearly see how her nipples tightened, thrusting against the filmy lace bra beneath her knit shirt. She made a mental vow to burn every knit shirt she owned.

His eyes lifted to meet hers in a smug, curious glance that made everything worse. Her body responded to Jared Calhoun. Without a touch or a word, with a mere look, he caused a reaction in her, and she didn't understand it. Usually she could maintain a chilly aloofness that discouraged attention quickly.

"Well, well," he said.

She glanced around as if seeking escape, and saw that they had reached a sprawling brown frame house, a driveway, a red pickup truck, a black Ford sedan, a brown barn, and a corral. Her relief was enormous. "We're home."

"So we are," he said without turning his head.

She let go of him and jumped down to the ground. He slipped off the horse with a groan and a few swear words. His face went white, his eyes narrowed, and she hurt for him. She took the reins from his hands, conscious of the slightest brush of their fingers.

"Let's go inside and bandage my foot," he said.

"We'll go to the hospital."

"You want me to bleed to death before I get there?" His blue eyes, now cold, rested on her.

"No, but I don't know anything about bandaging wounds."

"Give it your best."

She glared at his back as he turned away. He tried to walk on the heel of his injured foot and swore, his knees almost buckling. Courtney grabbed him and pulled his weight against her, causing *her* knees to almost buckle.

"Ready?" she said. As they moved together he ground his teeth and paled. "Can we do something else?" she asked.

"All right. Let me sit down. You put the horse in the corral. I shouldn't have dismounted here. Drive the truck close and help me get inside."

She glanced across the oak- and pine-shaded front yard that was fenced with split rails. "There's no way to get the truck here."

"Drive across the lawn, kid," he said slowly, as if he were talking to a three-year-old. He waved his hand. "Park right there a few feet away. Please, please don't run over me."

She led the horse to the corral, climbed into the truck, and gritted her teeth as she drove across the grass to him.

"Congratulations," he said as she knelt beside him, "you didn't hit me with the truck. Help me up, kid."

Grimly she slipped her arms around him, feeling a body that was muscular and fit.

"I used to run in track in college," he said. "Good thing we didn't meet then."

"I said I'm sorry. I just wanted to save Ebeneezer."

"I'm putting out a contract on Ebeneezer." He chuckled, and she burned. His face was only inches away, and his brown eyelashes were long, with a slight curl. Mr. Calhoun had bedroom eyes—when the glacial look was gone from his expression. She helped him into the truck and they drove to the gravel road that led to the highway.

"Who's your doctor, Mr. Calhoun?"

"Jared, kid. We're definitely on a first-name basis. It's an intimate relationship between the shooter and the shootee."

"Will you stop! I didn't shoot you. I accidentally caused you to shoot yourself, and if you'd been practicing gun safety that wouldn't have happened. Just another incident that shows how dangerous and unnecessary guns are."

"Oh, boy. You're one of those."

"And what's that supposed to mean?"

As she turned onto the highway they hit a bump. She heard him gasp and saw him clamp his jaw closed.

"I'm sorry. I didn't see the bump."

"Just keep your eyes on the road, and will you drive a little faster, please? Hell, I should've driven."

"And have you pass out at the wheel? No thanks!"

"We may get there tomorrow, or the next day, at this rate."

She stepped on the accelerator. "This is as dangerous as carrying a gun."

"Kid, pull over. Let me drive. I don't want to bleed to death ten minutes away from the hospital because you wouldn't go over a fifty-five-mile-an-hour speed limit."

"Pish-tosh."

"Pish what?"

She blushed. He was definitely laughing now! She saw his grin again and had the same instantaneous reaction.

"Kid, if you're at a loss for a good swear word, I—"

"Thank you, no! You're a vulgar man."

"You, Mrs. Meade, are a real prude. I'll bet that was some marriage."

She drew herself up and stared out the windshield, pressing the accelerator down even further. The sooner they reached the hospital, the quicker she could say good-bye to Mr. Jared Calhoun, and it was worth the risk of a speeding ticket to be done with him. No sooner had the thought crossed her mind than she heard a siren.

"Here's your chance," Jared said. "Go faster. His siren will clear the way."

"Not on your life!" She tightened her lips as she started to slow down.

"So I bleed to death to keep you from getting a ticket."

"Will you stop saying that!" She couldn't decide if he was teasing or not. She pulled off the road, momentarily hiding the patrol car in a cloud of dust that rose behind the truck.

The car halted behind her. A patrolman stepped out, approached them, and stopped beside the truck. Jared Calhoun leaned across the seat in his take-over fashion and said, "Officer, I'm bleeding. She shot me and I have to get to a hospital."

"Damn you!" she whispered.

"Such language!" Jared said with a frown.

"You don't look shot," the policeman said suspiciously, and stepped back, resting his hand on the butt of his gun.

"Come around to my side of the truck. It's my foot. She shot me in the foot."

"I did not, Officer!"

"Lady, get out of the truck."

"See what you've done." She opened the door and stepped down. As soon as the policeman spotted Jared's bleeding foot he swore.

"Domestic quarrel?"

"Yes, sir," Jared answered solemnly.

"I thought so," the patrolman said disgustedly. "Get in, lady. I'll lead the way to the hospital, and you follow."

"It's not what you think," she said.

"It never is. Get in." He sounded angry and tired.

She climbed in, gave Jared a furious glare, and waited while the policeman went back to his car.

"It wasn't a domestic quarrel," she said.

"What would you call it, open war?"

"You know what he meant by domestic. He meant a husband and a wife."

"I'll straighten him out later. It would take too long now. I tell you, kid, I may faint before much longer."

Shocked, she saw he was paler. Even though he acted as flinty as ever, he didn't appear quite so healthy. "You're just too ornery to faint."

He grinned. "Drive the truck. There he goes."

Two

Courtney swung onto the road behind the police car and suddenly they were barreling along at a speed she had never driven in her life. She clung to the wheel grimly.

"That's more like it," Jared said. "Hooray for the police. We'll get there today."

"Are you going to try to have me arrested?"

When he didn't answer, she turned her head and her heart lurched. Jared Calhoun was half turned toward her, studying her with speculation in his eyes. Speculation that was blatantly male. And the briefest glance conveyed a silent message.

"I might not." After two heartbeats of ominous silence he added darkly, "If I can be persuaded."

Courtney's heart dropped. She wouldn't put anything past Mr. Jared-Revolting-Calhoun. Nothing. He was as low-life as she had ever encountered in all her twenty-nine years. And not married. Her thoughts took a definite turn for the worse, and she felt a blush creep up her cheeks. She risked one more quick glance at him. He was so damned smug! Her worst fears were confirmed.

Anger and fear combined in a deadly mix. "What do I have to do?" she asked.

"You catch on fast, kid."

"Tell me what I have to do." She felt cold, then hot, then ill.

While she waited for Jared's answer, the police car reached town and they sped down a quiet street, vehicles moving out of the way. They threaded their way through the intersection, and Courtney concentrated fully on the car ahead of her.

She was terrified of the speed they were traveling. If a child ran in front of them, if a car didn't stop, she couldn't prevent a calamity. Mentally she swore at Jared Calhoun in words that he would have been completely familiar with.

They slowed at the hospital emergency entrance. The policeman parked and went inside immediately. Courtney braked to a jolting stop that sent her and Jared forward, then jerked them back.

He held up a thumb and forefinger in a neat circle. "We made it. Don't sign up for the Indy 'Five Hundred.' "

Attendants came out, and she was relieved to turn the care of Jared Calhoun over to someone else. Relieved, but not released. She followed them inside where she gave Jared's name, address, and insurance company, and when the blond nurse looked up and asked, "Are you his wife?" Courtney didn't mean to startle everyone behind the counter with her harsh, "Heaven forbid, no!"

She went to sit in the waiting room as the policeman directed, saying he would get her statement later. Vaguely, she wondered if she should call her best friend, Georgia, or if she should try to find a lawyer.

As she sat in the sunny waiting room she thought about the morning and Jared Calhoun. Her nerves felt as if she had been caught in a threshing machine. She knew what his request would be. The man probably couldn't get a date. She amended that. If he smiled he could, but she doubted if he smiled often. She fidgeted and tried to think of how to handle him, how to put him off without going to jail for causing his accident. He was the one with the gun. He was the one who had pulled the trigger. Surely they couldn't prosecute her for shooting him. She sighed, because she couldn't convince herself that she wasn't liable.

"Ahem!" A nurse stood in the doorway. "Would you like to see Mr. Calhoun now?"

Courtney wanted to answer no, that she never wanted to lay eyes on Jared Calhoun again, but she rose politely and followed the woman down the hall.

"The wound is superficial," the nurse said. "His foot is bandaged and he's resting comfortably now. You can take him home, probably not until tomorrow, though."

Courtney clenched her fists. She didn't want to take him home today, tomorrow, or any other time.

They entered a small emergency room. Jared was propped up on a narrow bed, looking as out of place as a snappish wolf. His tanned healthy skin, broad shoulders, and obvious muscles appeared incongruous against the white hospital sheets and pillows. His blue eyes met hers as the nurse cheerfully said, "Here she is!"

"I may need protection," he mumbled.

The nurse's eyes widened. "I beg your pardon? Did you say something, Mr. Calhoun?"

"I said I may get an infection."

The nurse smiled, patting his hand. "Oh, no. We take good care of our patients." She gave him a broad smile and smoothed his collar. "I'll take real good care of you, I promise."

Courtney realized the nurse was flirting with him. It came with as much shock as if she had discovered the nurse flirting with a sore-toothed grizzly.

Jared flashed one of his dazzling smiles and the nurse almost purred. She smoothed his covers, patted his pillow, then said to Courtney, "Ring if you want me." She smiled at Jared and left.

"You must have your moments," Courtney said.

His eyes settled on her like two angry hornets coming to rest. She felt as if one move, one breath, and she would be stung badly. Then she remembered their earlier conversation. "You won't press charges if I what?"

"That's one good thing, kid. You get right to the point."

"It's Courtney, not kid."

"Right, kid."

She gritted her teeth. "What's the condition?" She braced herself as she watched his gaze lower to her breasts. She wanted to ignore him, to look away, to feel nothing. How could this man, this strange, annoying, irritating, crusty man, make her quiver? she fumed. Beneath thin layers of skin, she was jelly.

A trial, jail, whatever lay ahead, she would not give in to his demand. The thought of Jared Calhoun's touch made her knees weak. She sat down in a chair.

Softly, he said, "One condition is all I ask."

His voice was husky, his face solemn, and she felt on fire. She loathed him, but her body couldn't work up the same distaste. There was a definite, unwanted chemistry, and it took nothing more than a glance from him to create spontaneous combustion!

"What is the condition?" She closed her eyes.

In breathy tones he said slowly, "I want you to give me . . . Ebeneezer."

It took thirty seconds for it to soak into her mind. She blinked, stared at him, and blinked again. "What?"

He grinned. "What did you think I wanted, kid? Your fair body?"

She blushed. From her throat, the heat rose in a suffocating, burning wave to her hairline. For a moment she hated Jared Calhoun. Never had anyone disturbed her, jolted her to such a degree.

"Kid," he said softly. "I wouldn't want to hurt your feelings, but I'm not that desperate."

She wanted to hit him. She had never in her life felt the urge even to slap a man. She had never understood fistfights or violence. Suddenly she understood fully. She looked at his straight nose and wanted to punch it. Or flatten the bedpan over his head.

"Nope, you're safe, kid. I'll bet you're as much fun in the sack as an icicle."

"And I'll bet you're as much fun as—" She snapped her mouth shut, trembling with rage.

"As what?"

"Never mind!"

"Just give me the bird." While he settled back smugly on the pillows, her mind shifted to what he had demanded.

"I can't give you Ebeneezer!"

His bristly jaw firmed. She saw the "or else" message in his stubborn expression. "You'd kill him!" she said.

"I would not only kill him, I would feed him to Admiral."

"I hate to ask, but who's Admiral?"

"Admiral Byrd. My Samoyed. A dog."

"I know that's a dog! You can't have Ebeneezer."

"The court usually goes easy on a woman. Wear a dress to the trial."

Burning with anger, she sat on her hands quickly, which he noticed. "Other than your horses," she said, "Ebeneezer hasn't ever harmed anyone or anything except prey that a hawk usually eats."

"Do tell. He's sent my horses into a dead run. They could've hurt themselves." He squinted at her. "That damned bird opened a gate!"

"Ebeneezer likes bright, shiny things." She wriggled beneath his glare. "Was the latch new?"

"Oh, damn. It took me days to find my horses. Do you know what a Tennessee Walking Horse is worth?"

"I have no idea."

"That buzzard has caused them to panic and almost injure themselves in the corral. He's mean and vicious."

"I can't imagine that. He's tame, but he does like shiny metal. If your horses had on bridles, something that caught his eye—"

"Don't make excuses for the bird. He should be a tasty meal once he's boiled. Kid, if you don't want to go to jail, give me that hawk!"

The door opened and a white-coated doctor entered the room. Jared settled back against the pillows. "This is Dr. Patterson," he said. "Dr. Patterson, this is the cause of it all, Mrs. Meade."

"How do you do?" The doctor gazed intently at her for a moment.

"Can I go home now?" Jared asked.

"You have someone at home to take care of you?"

"Yep. After four-thirty in the afternoon."

"No. All the time. I want you to stay off that foot

for the next few hours. If you don't have someone for the rest of the day, you should stay here."

"I need to get home. I have horses to feed."

Dr. Patterson turned to Courtney, and the moment he did, she knew what was coming. She felt a swift rush of joy. "You said Mrs. Meade is your neighbor. Perhaps she can stay until four-thirty?"

The question hung in the air. Courtney smiled at Jared Calhoun. "If Mr. Calhoun will agree to something."

Dr. Patterson waited while Jared stared at Courtney. Finally he shrugged one very broad shoulder.

"I agree. I know when someone's drawn a full house. Forget Ebeneezer."

"Yes, Dr. Patterson. I can take care of Mr. Calhoun until four-thirty."

The doctor seemed puzzled, then just shrugged. "Good. It's settled." He scratched out a prescription and handed it to Jared. "Take this as directed. Stay off that foot until tomorrow. You can get crutches downstairs. The wound is superficial, so it should heal quickly."

As he continued giving instructions to Jared, Courtney sank back in the chair. Relief overwhelmed her. He wouldn't press charges, she didn't have to hand over Ebeneezer, and all the dark imaginings running through her mind were nothing. By four-thirty, when it was time for Ryan to get home from school, she could go home. Until then, no one needed her.

Dr. Patterson left, the blond nurse returned, and Courtney, wondering what was the matter with the woman's taste in men, gladly let her bustle around Jared.

Within an hour they returned to Jared's house. He was using crutches, and Courtney helped him up the wooden steps, well aware of his lean frame pressed against her side. Her curiosity about his house mounted.

On the other side of the door, there was a scratching sound. "Admiral! Down, boy." Jared said. He opened the door and they stepped inside, and a white dog bounded at them, knocking them both flat. Jared yelped as he pitched forward, then fell on Courtney who'd tumbled onto her back. Her breath went out of her and she saw stars, bright, glittering lights. Something wet touched her cheek, and she looked up into dark happy eyes and a white face.

"I can't breathe," she gasped, and turned her head. Her lips grazed Jared's cheek. He stared at her, and for a moment time stopped. His blue eyes pinned her, and she became aware of every bit of her flesh pressed beneath Jared Calhoun's body. She felt his hard thighs against hers, his leg between hers, his hips pressing down, his broad chest crushing the breath from her lungs.

"Will you move!" she said, breathing with difficulty. He groaned and moved away, but it didn't ease the self-consciousness she felt.

"Get back, Admiral!" he commanded. The dog stepped back, then forward to touch Courtney with its paw. She patted its head, feeling the thick, soft fur.

"He's beautiful!" She wrapped her arms around his neck.

"Oh, kid, you've done it now. He loves to be petted. Get away, Admiral!"

The dog backed away a few feet and sat down. Courtney stood up and leaned down to help Jared. "He minds well."

"I don't want anything around that won't obey me."

"Including a woman," she said dryly, and

received a mocking grin that caused a flurry in her pulse.

"No, I like a woman who knows her own mind."

"Why do I find that hard to believe?"

"Knows her own mind is different from cantankerous and bashful as hell."

"I'm cantankerous?"

His grin diffused the accusation. "Only a smidge, kid."

"Cantankerous and bashful," she repeated. Suddenly she had to laugh. "The pot's calling the kettle black, Mr. Calhoun."

"Oh, kid, what a laugh you have!"

Warmth replaced laughter, and their relationship changed a fraction. Ignoring her own reaction, unable to understand the strange power that Jared Calhoun could effortlessly radiate, she moved closer and slipped her arm around him again, conscious of his warmth, his narrow waist, and the sharp thrust of his hipbone beneath the denim. When he was on his feet again, she paused and looked around the living room. It was all she had expected and worse.

Two wagon wheel light fixtures with brass lamps hung from the ceiling. Papers, magazines, fishing tackle, tools, and a stack of lumber littered the room. The heavy dark brown leather furniture was almost hidden beneath the mess, guns hung on the walls, the bookcases were haphazardly filled with books, and a wide stone fireplace was at one end of the room.

"Can you help me to bed?" Jared said.

Courtney almost jumped away. There was something in the way he asked that was too personal. She discovered that pesky twinkle in his eye.

"Of course," she said matter-of-factly.

"How long have you been divorced?"

"For eight years," she answered as she moved

with him, the two of them threading their way through the room. She was aware again of the chemistry between them.

"Sorry. That's rough, kid."

Surprised, she glanced up again. He had sounded as if he had meant what he said. Perhaps he wasn't as gruff as she had thought.

"How'd you get Ebeneezer?" he asked.

"He came to the sanctuary. He had an injured wing and I nursed him along. He stayed in the house for a time when he was young. He's really well-trained in some respects."

"He's mean as hell."

"He's very intelligent for a bird."

"Well, if I were you, kid, I'd sit down with Ebeneezer and have a person-to-bird talk. You say, 'Ebeneezer, old hawk, the guy next-door is going to kill you if you cross the property line. He will clean you and boil you and feed you to his big white dog, who will love every bite.' "

"Will you stop! That's disgusting."

"Here's my bedroom, kid," he drawled in a low voice. If he had intended to disturb her, he had succeeded. Courtney felt a tingle slither up her spine and diffuse in the back of her neck, leaving a residual trail of tiny sparks.

She glared at him, wishing she could fling him off and tell him to take care of himself. A glance confirmed her guess that his bedroom was as cluttered as the living room. Books, clothing, tools were scattered around the room. The four-poster bed was unmade, a gun rack and bookshelves covered one wall. She helped him to the bed, where he sat down and shook off his coat. She hung it in the closet and draped her own jacket over a chair.

"Now the first thing I need is a bath," Jared said.

"I'm not giving you a bath! That isn't what—"

She bit off the words when she saw his infuriating grin.

He laughed and winked. "Got you that time, kid. You're one straitlaced person. Need to learn to loosen up a little. How do you have fun? Go out and watch the birds fly?"

"You're a riot, Mr. Calhoun. A chuckle a minute," she said icily, watching the coolness melt under his grin. "If I go home, you'll have to go back to the hospital."

"No, I won't, and you can."

"Can what?"

"Go home."

"I promised Dr. Patterson."

"I won't hold you to it. You didn't promise me. I can get along fine right here by myself."

"Oh, no!" He wanted her to go, evidently. She wondered if he had teased her deliberately to get rid of her. "If something happened to you, I'd feel guilty. There's no way you can walk through this clutter without help. Here I am and here I stay, and if your man doesn't—"

"Who?"

"Guy, the man who works for you. Isn't that right?"

"What about him?" He tilted his head to one side and she had the uncomfortable feeling that he was holding back laughter.

"I'll stay until he comes, whenever that is."

Jared turned on his masculinity like someone throwing on a switch. His blue eyes focused on her intently, his lids lowered a fraction, his voice lowered a lot. "If necessary, you'd spend the whole night alone with me, kid?"

She felt like gnashing her teeth. How could one person stir such a violent response in another? She also couldn't ignore or understand that response. His throaty voice and penetrating gaze undid her. She shifted uncomfortably. She blushed and hated it. She tried to sound cold and stiff and unapproachable, but she knew her blush gave her away.

"I will if I have to," she said, "but I thought you said he comes at four-thirty."

"Bravery above and beyond the call," Jared murmured. "He'll come at four-thirty." He patted the bed. "Come here, kid, and tell me something."

"What?"

"Sit beside me," he coaxed in a voice that sent sparks snapping in her veins.

"No."

"Scared?"

She shot him a look and was caught. His voice dropped another notch to a fuzzy depth that stroked her senses with a velvety softness.

"You're scared. I don't think you're twenty-nine. I think you tell people that to protect yourself."

"I'm twenty-nine all right. And I'm not scared of you, Jared Calhoun." She sat beside him on the bed. He took her wrist in his hand, and it was seconds before she realized he was taking her pulse. She tried to slip her arm free, but his fingers firmed.

"You'll stay here all night with me if I'm alone tonight—if Guy doesn't come?"

"I will, and don't get ideas!"

"Kid, you're cute, but I don't make love to babes in arms."

She fumed silently as she gazed into his eyes. He was an adult male and attractive— That word made her mental train of thought jolt to a stop. Jared Calhoun, attractive? He looked down at her wrist, and Courtney assessed him, taking note of his thick brown hair that had a wave to it and curled above his ears, his prominent cheekbones, his strong jaw that needed a shave, his neck that appeared about a size sixteen, the breadth of his shoulders and chest. Dark hair curled at the open neck of his knit shirt. The short sleeves banded muscled arms. A snug belt with a wide gold-colored buckle circled a narrow waist, and the jeans were molded to lean hips. She raised her eyes.

"What's your opinion?" he asked.

He had been watching her! she realized. Courtney felt on fire and knew there was no way to stop her blush. When she tried to jerk her arm out of his grasp, his fingers tightened slightly holding her. She refused to get into a real contest with him. She quit struggling immediately and glared at him.

"I . . ." She couldn't think of one thing to answer.

He grinned. "Maybe you're not so straitlaced after all. That survey wasn't. And your opinion must be too hot to tell. Damn well set your pulse racing. Kid, you're cute when you get riled up."

She shook with anger. The "kid" tag was beginning to grate. She wanted Mr. Jared Calhoun to take her seriously, if for no other reason than to put a little respect into him.

"Will you let go?"

"Stay a minute."

"I'd have thought you'd be sufficient unto yourself."

"I like a little company now and then. Are you hungry?"

"No, but I'll get you something."

"Good. I'm so hungry I could eat a hawk." Startled, she looked up, and he laughed.

"That isn't funny."

"Just a little jab at Ebeneezer. Where'd he get the cute name?"

"You don't like the name Ebeneezer when you have a dog named Admiral Byrd?"

"I think 'Admiral Byrd' has a good ring to it. It

has dignity. It makes you think of white snow, and a Samoyed makes you think of an icy winter. But Ebeneezer?"

"He likes to save things."

"Oh, Scrooge. This ought to be good. A hawk who likes to save things? What kind of things, baby chickens?"

"I can see we don't have the same sense of humor, Mr. Calhoun."

"You mean you don't have a sense of humor."

His gibe hurt, because he was hitting close to a sensitive area. As much as she had always wanted to be easygoing and relaxed, it just wasn't her nature. She answered stiffly, "Ebeneezer likes little bits of shiny metal, buttons, coins, things like that. He brings them home to his box."

"Isn't a hawk a damned weird pet? Do you hold him in your lap and pet him?"

"Of course not. He lights on the kitchen window, and I talk to him, and—" She saw the expression on Jared Calhoun's face and snapped her mouth shut. "I'll see what I can get you to eat."

She easily found the kitchen, which had brown oak cabinets and counters littered with empty cans, flowerpots, vases, papers, and tools. In addition to the clutter, there was a wagon wheel light fixture hanging over the table, rust-colored chintz curtains at the windows, and brown braided rugs on the floor. Gleaming copper pans hung on one wall. In spite of the disarray, there were no dusty corners, no dirty dishes. Jared Calhoun's house was clean chaos.

She heard the cold north wind howl around a corner of the building. She thought about Ryan at school and wondered if he had enough warm clothes for the walk from the bus stop to the house. She could picture his big gray eyes, the blond hair peeking out from beneath his red woolen cap, his thin body wrapped in jeans, boots, and a blue parka. He should be warm enough, she told herself.

It occurred to her that if she told Jared Calhoun about her son and how attached Ryan was to Ebeneezer, it would appeal to the man. Surely he had kindness in him somewhere. The phone rang, and she glanced around. It must be hidden by papers or tools. It rang again, then stopped, and she assumed Jared had answered an extension.

When she opened the refrigerator, she drew a sharp breath. The top shelf held bottles of beer and soda pop. The second shelf was filled with jars of peppers and packages of cheese, the third shelf was full of large cuts of raw beef, including four thick steaks.

She began to search in earnest, opening a bread box to find only rye bread, opening the pantry to find an assortment of ketchup, cans of sauerkraut, jars of jalapeño peppers, chowchow, and pickled peppers. She searched all through the food supply, then went back to the bedroom.

Jared Calhoun was lying back against the pillows, a thick cigar clenched in his teeth, a magazine in his hands. He lowered the magazine when he heard her approach.

"That was Guy who called," he said. "He'll be a little late, but you can go home now, kid, if you like."

"No. I told you I'd stay. When does Guy expect to get here?"

"He's my son." Jared grinned and carefully extinguished his cigar.

"My goodness!"

"Yep, kid, once I was married. I'm widowed now. That was Guy calling to tell me that the school bus will be late."

"Then Ryan will be late."

"Who's Ryan?"

"My son. He's in school, and if the school bus doesn't leave at the regular time—" She stopped at the surprise in Jared's expression.

"Kid, you're a mother!"

She knew she was in for another inspection, which he conducted as leisurely as before. She felt his gaze lower slowly over her figure, as if he were using his hands instead of his eyes. His look was blatantly sexual, obvious, and intense enough to generate its own heat.

She drew in her breath, then too late realized it made her breasts thrust against her shirt, stretching the white knit tautly. Jared's gaze rose to her eyes.

She blushed, she quivered. She wanted to fling her hands in front of her. She wanted to ask him, "Do you want to say 'kid' now?" Instead, she stood still and waited. "Are you through?" she asked aloud.

"No," he said softly. "No. You want to know what I'd really like to do?"

"No!"

He smiled. "You're scared, kid. How'd you ever get married and have a son? What kind of man was he?"

"He wasn't like you," she said icily. The last thing on earth she wanted to discuss with Jared Calhoun was her marriage. He continued to look at her, and she felt nailed to a wall beneath a glaring probe that could shine into her soul. He was silent a moment, then asked, "Where's your son go to school?"

"Jefferson Davis Elementary."

"I'll be damned. How old is he?"

"Nine."

"So's Guy. I haven't heard him mention Ryan Meade, but we've only lived here a short time now."

"And I haven't heard Ryan mention your son, but Ryan keeps to himself. He's a little shy."

"Like his mother," Jared said with a chuckle. She turned to go to the kitchen, remembered what she had been doing, and turned back around. "Is that all the food you have?"

"Yeah. There's plenty for us to eat. You want more than four steaks?"

"There's nothing to drink except beer and soda pop!"

"Oh, boy. Try and keep the lecture to a minimum." He closed his eyes.

"You have a nine-year-old son. What does he drink?"

"Soda pop. Won't stunt his growth. He's almost as tall as you are."

"Oh, my heavens!"

He opened his eyes and grinned. "I'm surprised you didn't say, 'Oh, drat it.' "

"Well, that's disgusting!"

"Kid, don't tell me one more time that I'm disgusting."

She felt on fire with anger. This obnoxious man was like a burr beneath a bare foot. And to add to it, he was ordering her around now as if he owned her. She spoke as slowly and clearly as he had earlier.

"Mr. Calhoun, you are very disgusting— loathesome, irritating, and disgusting. A man who would let a nine-year-old child have a steady diet of soda pop is disgusting; your smelly old cigar is disgusting; your foul language is disgusting."

Jared's blue eyes became icy. He sat up straighter, then swung his feet over the side of the bed. Suddenly Courtney was thankful he couldn't walk. She took a step backward, realized he had intimidated her with a mere look, and stopped.

"You can't put your weight on your foot. Get back into bed, Mr. Calhoun."

"You know, kid, I can't think of any woman in my adult life who has ordered me around or provoked me as much as you have! Now, I warned you . . ."

Courtney's heart lurched, but she stood still. Beside her knee Admiral Byrd growled.

"Admiral!" Jared roared, and the dog slumped down and put his nose between his front paws.

Amused, Courtney knelt down. Admiral sat up and put his paw on her knee while she hugged him and his tail thumped on the floor. "Oh, sweet doggie, has the mean old man scared you?" She gave Jared a triumphant smile.

"I should've named him Judas instead of Admiral."

"He knows a nice person when he sees one."

"Bull," Jared said, but it looked as if his eyes had developed a twinkle.

"And he knows a disgusting one when he sees one."

"That does it—"

"You can't get up! Lie down and I'll get you a beer." Laughing softly, she left the room with Admiral at her heels.

When she reached the kitchen, Admiral scratched at the door. She let him out and watched him bound across the yard, then got a bottle of beer, opened it, and returned to the bedroom. When she stepped inside, the door slammed shut behind her.

Three

Courtney saw the empty bed at the same moment she heard the door slam. Her heart jumped, and she spun around.

A strong arm closed around her, and Jared took the beer from her hand and set it on a table.

"Mr Calhoun!"

"Relax, I won't bite," he said. "Not hard, that is." One corner of his mouth rose in a mocking grin, and her pulse skyrocketed. His voice was at a velvety level that invaded her senses. "Now, kid, you're not going to call me disgusting again."

"I won't," she said quickly, and it came out in such a whisper, she was sure he didn't hear her.

"Closer," he demanded.

"No!" she said in a panicky tone as she tried to wriggle free. He frowned, watching her curiously while he tightened both arms around her. His chest was like a solid wall, and he held her steadfast, pressing her hard to his body as his head dipped down to brush his lips across hers.

She had feared and expected force, a bruising kiss, as commanding as his other actions. He should have been rough and forceful when he kissed, she thought, but he wasn't. Not at all.

Instead it was the merest touch. His breath, which held the slightest trace of tobacco and mint, mingled with hers momentarily. The kiss was so light, so gently careful, as if she were a very fragile rose that needed warmth to open. Never had she been kissed in such a way.

When he paused, she gazed up at blue eyes that had darkened, that made her knees weak with their inquisitiveness.

"Kid, I may have misjudged you as much as you misjudged me." His voice was rough, husky, and low. His head lowered, and he brushed her lips again faintly, yet it caused a chain reaction.

Her mouth tingled, and for the first time in so long, heat radiated downward. Her blood became sluggish and hot. She tipped her head back to peer up at him through a fringe of blond lashes, and the expression on his face took the last bit of breath she had.

He put his hand behind her head, spread his fingers, and drew her face to him while he watched her. Her lips parted. She couldn't breathe, she felt hot, and she wanted his kiss. Beyond reason, the man who had annoyed her so fiercely since morning was now so exciting that she couldn't draw her breath.

She leaned toward him. Surprise and something unknown flared in the depths of his eyes. "Son-of-a-gun!" he whispered, then settled his lips firmly over hers, opening her mouth wide to a questing invasion by his tongue, taking and giving and changing their relationship another notch.

And never again would she call Jared Calhoun disgusting. He had proved his point beyond a shadow of a doubt. She was stunned by the reaction he had caused as she trembled in his arms. She heard him groan and wondered if he had forgotten and put his weight on his foot. His foot! He shouldn't be out of bed . . . bed . . . and Jared . . . Her thoughts swirled, and she felt as if she were tumbling down, beyond the Looking Glass to Wonderland, to a wonderland of sensation. A wonderland of something that had been dormant till now. It had never been like this. It seemed so right now. So very, very right.

She could smell the clean scent of Jared's clothes. She slipped her hands over his shoulders and felt the bulge of hard muscle. An arm tightened around her, and she pressed against the length of his fit body. His stubbly jaw scraped her skin.

When he raised his head, he looked shocked. She herself felt stunned beyond imagination. He stroked her cheek lightly. "Who tied you up in knots, kid? Was it your ex-husband?" he asked softly.

"No, I'm just not a relaxed type." Startled by his probing question, she tried to think of something else to say. "You shouldn't be out of bed," she whispered, tilting her face up as she talked.

"You shouldn't kiss like that," he whispered in return. "It defies all reason. . . ." He gazed at her lips, his dark fringe of lashes coming down to hide his eyes.

"You better sit down," she said, but she wasn't certain what she'd said. This crusty, gruff man was as sensitive to others as a daisy to sunshine, she realized.

"Yeah, I know. My foot's killing me."

"Want me to help you to bed?"

"Oh, yeah," he said, so sincerely, she felt on fire. She trembled again, and his arms tightened.

"You're trembling," he said.

"No, I'm not," she denied, even as she clung to him. She didn't know if she was or not.

"Yes, you're shaking," he murmured, and with each word his lips came closer, then touched hers again.

This kiss shattered the earlier record, as shock waves from it registered higher on her heart's scale. Courtney felt warmth low in her belly, and it spread like heated honey, licking into her veins to scorch, to make her hips shift with need, thrusting against his hardness, seeking—

Shocked, she pushed away, staring at him as if he had dropped to earth from the heavens. Her breathing was irregular, causing an erratic rise and fall of her full breasts.

"I'll get your lunch," she said shakily.

His chest expanded and narrowed with his breath. "Will you help me back to bed?" he asked, his voice deep and fuzzy.

"Ahh . . ."

"I won't kiss you."

She blinked. Was his promise a relief—or a disappointment? There had been something so right about being in his arms, as if she belonged there. Again startled, she blanked out her questions.

Before his kisses physical contact with him had been quite noticeable to her. Now, it felt as if she were dallying around a hot, rumbling volcano. Each brush of his body, his hip, his hand, seared raw nerves and struck a chord of response that was invisible yet tangible.

While she drew her breath, steeled herself, and slipped an arm around his waist to help him to bed, she was again aware of his thorough scrutiny.

"How did you get across the room by yourself?" she asked.

"I managed." He turned, and his mouth was inches away. "Kid, how you had a son is beyond me. Well, maybe not completely beyond me. Those were damned nice kisses. Better than nice. . . ."

"Mr. Calhoun! Will you stop analyzing our kisses!"

"Kid, you're a prude."

"And you're a raunchy, crusty coot!" she snapped back defensively, but her voice held a lightness that belied her accusation.

He chuckled. "Raunchy, crusty coot. You're getting better. Stick around a while and you'll be able to swear with the best of us." His teasing laughter took the bite out of his words.

The old phrase "all bark and no bite" came to her mind. Was Jared all bark? Only crusty on the surface? she wondered. His kisses had held no cruel demands, only the most honeyed coaxing.

They reached the bed, and he sat down, then grimaced and drew a sharp breath. His hands fell on her arms casually.

"Oh, damn that hurt!"

"I'm sorry."

He opened his eyes briefly, then closed them, squinting tightly as if in deep pain.

"How long since the last pain pill?" she asked.

"An hour. I have to wait awhile before I take another." He spread his knees apart and drew her closer to the bed.

"Ohhh!" he gasped.

"Oh, dear! I'm sorry you're in such pain."

"Oh, kid, hold me!"

He wrapped his arms around her and placed his head against her breasts, and Courtney held him, stroking his back, conscious of his hot breath burning through her clothes.

His voice was a low rumble. "Mmmm, you smell nice. You're soft."

She opened her eyes wide. He hadn't sounded in pain at all! She pulled away so swiftly, he almost fell off the bed. He swore and scooted back.

"You don't hurt!" she said.

He had the grace to look guilty, and somehow, when he did, he became less formidable, and she bit back a smile. She moved away to get his beer, stretching her arm out to hand it to him.

He gave her a mocking smile, and she stepped closer to the bed. "What would you like for lunch," she asked, "cheese and beer or peppers and beer?"

"Oh, my, the disapproval! You need a tambourine and a street corner for the lecture. Don't give one here."

"Mr. Calhoun—"

"I'm gonna get it anyway." He closed his eyes and sank down on the propped-up pillows, but Courtney wasn't deterred.

"I don't care if you eat elm leaves and drink muddy water, but soda pop and hot peppers are a terrible diet for a little boy!"

"The little boy is healthy as a horse."

"Be that as it may, he needs some vitamins." She stuck to her lecture, but beneath it all ran the current of her awareness of Jared Calhoun stretched out in his big bed.

"There are vitamins in steak, cheese, and bread," Jared said, "and he eats half his meals at school."

"He probably smokes and chews."

Jared's eyes opened. "He did chew, but he stopped."

She drew a deep breath and shuddered, causing Jared to laugh. "Relax, kid. I don't chew."

Startled, she blinked and stared at him. How had he known what she was thinking?

He chuckled again and continued. "Guy's promised he won't do it. It was just a boyish experiment," he added quietly, and blushed. She had struck a nerve, she realized, the man did have a grain of sense.

"It's still poor eating," she said. "I'm amazed that living on cheese and beer, you're so—" She realized what she was about to say and snapped her mouth shut. Where was her brain?

She wasn't going to get off the hook this time. As his eyes opened wide her cheeks burned. He grinned his orneriest son-of-a-gun grin and said, "Go on, don't leave me in suspense. I'm so what?"

"What would you like for lunch, Mr. Calhoun?"

"When you get your feathers ruffled, you get very stiff and formal." His voice dropped to that intimate huskiness that made her pulse jump. "I'm so what? The possibilities are mind-boggling!"

"Well, put your mind at rest!" She decided to end the conversation and get out of it before he made matters worse. Which he seemed to have a real knack for doing. "With a steady intake of beer and cheese, I'm amazed you're so strong."

The creases in his cheeks appeared as annoyingly appealing as ever while his blue eyes smirked.

"That isn't what you were going to say, kid."

"Yes, it was!"

"Sure 'nuff."

"Mr. Calhoun, do you want lunch?"

He folded his hands over his chest and developed an air of innocence, except for his eyes. They were as devilish as Old Nick's. "Yeah, kid. I'm starving. I want . . ." He stared at her lips and licked his.

"Will you stop?"

His dark brows arched. The soul of innocence asked, "Stop what? I was getting ready to tell you what I want."

"Do you think we'll get the menu by noon tomorrow?"

He laughed. "Keep your bonnet strings tied. I'll have cheese and peppers on rye, and a beer. Feel free to toss one of those steaks in the broiler if you don't like cheese."

"I love cheese!"

"Bet you don't love beer."

"How astute."

"How as—what?"

"You know what I said. Should you drink beer when you're taking pain pills?" The moment she said it, she saw his grin. "I'm sure you're too crusty for it to matter!"

At the door she paused. "Mustard or mayonnaise?"

He shook his head. "None on the premises. Sorry. Try some peppers. You'll never miss the mustard." He squinted at her. "Bet you don't eat hot peppers either."

"No, I don't."

"Might thaw you out."

She smiled at him frostily and left with his chuckle floating in the air behind her.

She fixed the sandwiches, heaping hot peppers on his, poured a glass of ice water, and heard him call to bring another beer. She returned to the bedroom and placed a tray of food in front of him. She was conscious of his gaze resting on her as she moved around him.

"Thanks, kid, you're a real help."

"You're welcome, Mr. Calhoun."

His eyes twinkled as he settled back to eat. "Now, this is good. I'll bet your sandwich is as dry as the desert."

"It's fine."

"Have you lived next door long?"

"For two hundred years."

He coughed and smiled. "The old family place?"

She nodded. "Yes, my ancestors settled here when it was a wilderness."

"And since then you've kept it that way?"

"No, it was a farm for years until my grandfather died. Before my father's death, my parents donated one hundred and ten acres to Nashville, and the city declared it a nature sanctuary. In return, I now have a plot of land where my home is. I get paid a small pension for showing groups through, for living there."

"You don't have to take care of everything, do you?"

"No, the city maintains most of the sanctuary. I'm enrolled in correspondence courses toward a degree in zoology."

His brows raised. "That must keep you busy."

"I like it. Nature's a fascinating subject, and the sanctuary can be developed in so many ways."

"Is it a nature sanctuary or just for birds?"

"Mostly birds, but we call it a nature sanctuary because we have small animals, rabbits, possums, squirrels," she answered, marveling at how easy he could be to talk to. "There are turtles, fish, and snakes in the pond. We have nature trails and a small exhibit building, three creeks and the pond that extends over onto your land." After a moment she asked him, "How long has your wife been gone?"

"Thirteen months. It was a malignancy."

"I'm sorry."

He had said it quietly, yet, because of her own grandmother's illness, she understood all that it meant. The pain, the worries, and the slow heartbreak.

They ate their sandwiches while a comfortable silence filled the room. It was a full ten minutes later when he looked up at her. "Kid, I'm glad you don't mind a little quiet now and then."

She smiled. "I was an only child. I've spent lots of time alone in my life. I enjoy quiet." The doorbell rang, and she stood up. "I'll see who it is."

At the door she was surprised to find three of the bird-watchers had come to ask after Jared. She asked them to wait and returned to the bedroom.

"It's some of my bird-watchers," she said. "They've come to see if you're all right."

"Send them in."

"They're sweet people."

"So am I."

"Funny man." She left and ushered the three people into Jared's bedroom.

"Mr. Calhoun, I'd like you to meet Henry Twilling, Mrs. Jones, and Miss Barnhill."

"Push the books aside and sit down, folks. Nice of you to drop by. We're just sitting here having a beer."

"We weren't!"

"Would anyone care for a beer?"

All three declined. "How're you feeling now, Mr. Calhoun?" Miss Barnhill asked.

"I'm doing fine with the help of the kid, here."

Three heads turned to look at Courtney, and she blushed.

"Is there anything we can do?" Henry Twilling asked.

"Naw, thanks. It's nice of you people to come by and call. Especially under the circumstances. You know, I'm almost glad about this injury." He focused on Courtney, and she mentally braced for the next onslaught. It came.

"Kid and I wouldn't have gotten to know each other otherwise. At least not so intimately so quickly."

Her skin was as irritating as Jared Calhoun. She

could feel it turn red. She laughed weakly. "We've had a nice conversation about our sons. Mr. Calhoun has a son the same age as mine." She was chattering, Jared was grinning, and the three guests were staring.

"Yeah, it's been some day. Kid's been bustling and fussing over me like a hen with one chick. You folks love little birds?"

"We have some interesting varieties here," Henry Twilling said, warming to his subject. "A golden-crowned kinglet winters in the sanctuary, there are bluebirds all year, yellow-throated vireos in the summer. Matter-of-fact, last March a rough-winged swallow was spotted, the earliest we've recorded, so we're hoping to see another one this March."

"Well, do tell. I haven't seen any bluebirds, but I have a long-eared owl that's been around here this winter and when the weather was warm, I saw a scissor-tailed flycatcher down by my pond," Jared said, his southern drawl deepening.

"Goodness, that's the second time someone has spotted a scissor-tailed flycatcher in this area!" Henry said.

Shocked, Courtney gazed at Jared. When had he taken time to learn to identify birds? she wondered. He looked like the last person on earth to know one bird from another except to hunt. He was talking blithely on the subject, smiling at her smugly.

"And believe it or not," he continued, "I've spotted a house finch."

"A house finch!" Courtney exclaimed. "There aren't any in this part of the country."

"Oh, yes. I saw one at the pond. No mistaking it either. I took a picture of it."

"You did?"

"Yep. I'll have to find it."

She was discussing birds with him! Courtney blinked and closed her mouth while Jared smiled at her. And she returned his smile. For a moment they had a common interest and stood on common ground, and it was nice.

Henry said, "How interesting. Courtney, I heard that Jeff Reardon saw a house finch on his place."

"I didn't know that," she answered absentmindedly, her thoughts elsewhere. Jared Calhoun was a complex man. What made him so ill-natured? she wondered. He seemed to know as much about birds as anyone in the room, he was sensitive, perceptive, exciting . . . and so annoying! She glanced out the window and her heart jumped.

Ebeneezer was perched on the window ledge! She drew a deep breath and studied Jared, who was still talking. Her gaze moved from his foot to the gun rack, and she was thankful he couldn't run. Then she noticed Miss Barnhill watching her curiously.

Courtney slowly lifted her hand and placed her finger over her lips in a signal for silence from Miss Barnhill. She turned and then jumped as she looked into Jared Calhoun's curious blue eyes.

Four

"Yep, I haven't seen a yellow vireo since I moved in here," Jared was saying, but his full attention was on Courtney. She could see the speculation in his gaze. She looked down at her lap and prayed that he wouldn't glance out the window.

"Can I get you another beer?" she asked him. Maybe with the pain pill and the beer he'd pass out.

He thought it over. "No, thanks. I'm fine."

"Would anyone like a glass of water?" She stood up, intending to go out and shoo Ebeneezer away. "If you'll excuse me! Miss Barnhill, tell Mr. Calhoun about the time we found the crane with the injured leg."

Miss Barnhill seemed startled, then she frowned. "Oh, well, we found a crane with an injured leg . . ." Courtney escaped and immediately went out the back door. Instantly, as if they had both seen her coming, Admiral bounded up, almost knocking her over, and Ebeneezer swooped out of the sky to land on her shoulder, his talons fastening securely.

She waved her hand at him. "Ebeneezer, go home!"

He ruffled his wing, batted her on the head, but remained on her shoulder. Admiral sat down, wagging his tail as if he were laughing. Desperately, she picked up the bird with care, well aware of how sharp his talons were. "Ebeneezer, do you want Admiral to eat you?"

She felt guilty. Admiral was too sweet to harm anything. "Do you want that nasty man to shoot you? Go home." She tossed the bird into the air.

With a squawk, he turned and swooped down to light on her shoulder again.

"Ebeneezer!" Courtney was aware of time passing, time in which she couldn't see what Jared was doing. She could picture him suddenly appearing. In spite of his injury, he had a way of getting around when he wanted to. She could imagine him with a pistol, finishing Ebeneezer off, right on her shoulder!

"Go home!" With a flap, Ebeneezer rose and sailed through the open door into Jared Calhoun's house!

Courtney ran inside and Admiral followed. The bird flew to the wagon wheel chandelier in the kitchen and perched on it, making it swing crazily.

"Ebeneezer," she whispered, her heart thudding, "come down. He'll kill you. You're in the house of a man who wants to cook you!"

The hawk's beady black eyes glittered, and he clung to the swinging wagon wheel. Courtney got a piece of bread and held it up. Ebeneezer fluffed his feathers and stared at the bread.

She pulled out a kitchen chair. "Please come down. He'll cook you and eat you, and Ryan and I will cry. He'll wring your neck and put you in a pot and boil you. You are in the home of an ornery man who detests you," she said in a low voice, glancing nervously at the door while she climbed onto the chair.

She was at eye level with the hawk, who watched her impassively. She held the bread with one hand and reached for him with the other.

Suddenly he was gone, the chandelier swinging and almost toppling Courtney off the chair.

"Drat it!" She watched with a sinking feeling as Ebeneezer flew through the kitchen door into the hall. Her heart thumped rapidly. It was important to save the bird. How would she explain to Ryan that their neighbor had cooked his pet hawk? She climbed down and hurried into the living room.

Ebeneezer was perched on another wagon wheel light fixture. From the direction of the bedroom Courtney heard voices, several voices, as if they were getting ready to leave. She prayed for time, for Ebeneezer to fly out the door, for Jared to stay in bed. She hurried across the room and opened the front door. "Get out!" she said in a whispery rush.

Ebeneezer pecked at one of the lamps, his beak making a sharp ringing noise as it hit the metal.

"I don't want to tell Ryan you were boiled. Go!" She heard the voices approaching. They were coming! She thought she heard Jared's voice. She did hear the thump of crutches, then the guests and their host appeared.

Jared's gaze drifted upward, and he began to swear so violently that Miss Barnhill turned scarlet and rushed to the door.

"We have to go now," she said.

Ebeneezer, with the aplomb of one on center stage, flapped his wings and settled on Jared's head.

The swearing became a roar as Jared dropped a crutch and reached for the bird.

"Ebeneezer!" Courtney cried.

The hawk sailed into the air and out the front door. Jared hobbled on one crutch to a gun cabinet, fished a key from his pocket, and unlocked the case.

"Don't shoot my hawk!" Courtney said.

"Oh, my goodness!" Mrs. Jones said.

Jared produced a black pistol. The sight of it made Courtney turn to ice. She ran to block the door while Mr. Twilling and Mrs. Jones scooted close together.

Jared turned, slipping a clip into the gun. The click was loud in the silence. Courtney drew herself up and put her hands on her hips, blocking the doorway as he came across the room. Once again she was thankful he was on one foot. Otherwise, she wouldn't stand a chance. She glanced swiftly over her shoulder but couldn't spot Ebeneezer, and prayed he had flown home.

Then he squawked, and she knew he was terribly, dangerously, close at hand.

"Don't shoot him! He's my son's pet."

Jared's blue eyes developed a determined glint and a suspicious twinkle. "Get out of my way, kid."

"Not on your life!"

"Won't be on my life."

Each step closer he came, her pulse jumped drastically. She didn't want a showdown with Jared Calhoun. Even though he was wounded and limping, he still held a loaded gun, and he was formidable enough without a weapon.

"Don't shoot my pet! I'll put him in a cage and keep him home!"

"Why do I doubt that?"

"I don't like guns."

"I don't like Ebeneezer."

"Please . . ."

He stopped inches away, and his gaze went past her. "That damned bird landed right on my head!"

His strong tanned fingers held the weapon pointed at the floor, but it still looked ugly and deadly. She gulped and said, "I hate, loathe, and despise guns, and you have one only inches from me."

"The safety's on. I have it pointed at the floor. Get out of my way, kid. That damned bird is out there somewhere. I heard him squawk."

Suddenly there was a flapping of wings.

For lack of something better to do, Courtney threw her arms around Jared, pinning his own arms and his crutch to his side, and kissed him.

For one millisecond, she caught him by surprise. Then, in spite of the hold she had on him, he took charge. Completely. His mouth opened, settling firmly on hers, and his tongue thrust between her lips in a brazen, masculine assertion that was as delicious as it was cavalier.

He kissed her deeply, thoroughly, and to such an extent she forgot everything else: Ebeneezer, the onlookers, the loaded gun. Everything except Jared Calhoun.

His kiss was outrageously spectacular, she thought. It should have been against all laws for such an arrogant, rascally man to kiss with the sparkle and zest of vintage champagne.

He raised his head, and his gaze compelled her full attention. She couldn't breathe. The room was suffocating, and her pulse was drumming like hailstones on a car roof.

"I'm gonna put a bullet right through his heart," he said softly, and leaned down to kiss her again.

She let him. It was better than letting him shoot Ebeneezer. A whole lot better.

He was warm and solid. He felt right, as if she

had been created to fit perfectly into his arms. His kisses were right too—something that should have been impossible.

Jared shifted his weight. They exchanged positions as his arms wrapped around her. For a man who could stand on only one foot, he did remarkably well.

When he raised his head again, she felt stunned. He gazed beyond her; she heard a flapping of wings, remembered what was happening, and turned around to see Ebeneezer flying toward the sanctuary.

As her gaze lowered to Miss Barnhill's open mouth and raised eyebrows, heat flooded Courtney's face. Mrs. Jones's face was red, and Mr. Twilling was staring at her intently. "We'll run along now," he said.

Within seconds she had closed the door behind them and turned to face Jared Calhoun, who now blocked her path.

She tried to pull some semblance of normalcy into the situation. "You're supposed to stay off your foot," she said.

"Yeah, I know." He propped himself on his good foot and crutch, reaching out with his hand to take hold of her braid.

"Long golden hair," he said softly, his words like mist drifting over her in fine, light touches. "You think fast. You're kinda fun, kid. Can't say you're run-of-the-mill."

"Thanks. You aren't run-of-the-mill either," she said dryly, making him chuckle, while something inside her warmed from his praise. "Will you turn around? I'll help you back to bed."

"That's a deal, kid," he said huskily. He held out his arm, and she slipped her own arm around his narrow waist, the touch a searing contact.

"You smell nice," he said.

"Thank you." She was aware of each brush of his hip against hers as they walked, of his arm pressing on her shoulders.

"Will you put my gun away, please?" he asked when they reached his room.

"Oh, yes."

He chuckled. "Forgot all about it, didn't you?"

He hadn't changed, she thought. He was as ornery as ever. "I might've forgotten for a moment. I told you, I don't like guns."

"But you sure as hell like to kiss. You're some kisser, kid."

She blushed fiery red and wished she could stop.

"Sends my temperature soaring. I might get well faster if we keep it up."

"Forget it!"

"My, you're touchy about something you have a real natural talent for. I mean—"

"Mr. Calhoun! I'm going home!" He could get along by himself. He would survive. He was as tough as cactus.

"Okay, kid. Would you please put the gun away before you go? You can let Admiral in again."

While she was extricating herself from Jared Calhoun, she realized he was happy to see her go. He didn't want her underfoot, probably he was very self-sufficient. She went to the living room, put the gun in the cabinet, and returned to the bedroom.

"I won't let you run me off until four-thirty," she said. "I keep my promises, and I promised that doctor I'd stay and see that you're all right."

He was propped against the pillows again, a magazine in his hands. He put it down, turned on his hip carefully, and patted the bed.

"Want to make time fly?"

"No!" She came in and sat down in the chair, ignoring her blush and his amusement. "Let's settle this."

"Settle what, that you can really kiss?"

"Will you stop talking about bed and kisses!"

"I don't recall saying one word about bed. Freudian slip there, kid."

She closed her eyes and counted to ten. "I want to talk seriously with you."

"I'll talk seriously. I'll kiss seriously. I'll talk and kiss—"

"Mr. Calhoun!"

He grinned. "Okay, get it off your chest, kid. What's bugging you?"

He could swing so quickly from treating her as a sexy, appealing woman to talking to her as if she were an eight-year-old child, from teasing banter to earnest conversation, that Courtney couldn't keep up with the changes. "I want to discuss Ebeneezer," she said.

"Discuss the bird, kid. I'm all ears."

"He's part of the family. My son has had a rocky time without a father."

"That I can imagine."

His gibe struck a sensitive area and hurt. With an effort she continued. "And Ebeneezer is important to Ryan."

"If you'll send Ryan over, I'll teach him to ride."

She blinked in surprise. The thought of Ryan with Jared Calhoun and a younger version of him sent a chill down her spine. "Thank you, that's nice, but . . ."

His grin widened. "But you don't want your precious sonny within ten miles of me."

"Well, if you put it so bluntly, yes." She sat up straighter, growing irritated again. "Thanks, anyway. Now can we discuss Ebeneezer? School will be out shortly and I can go home."

"Sure. Go ahead and talk. Don't you want a beer? It might relax you."

"No, thanks. Ebeneezer is very important. I'm

sorry if he's bothering your horses, although it's hard to imagine. Nevertheless, if he is, we'll pen him up for a time."

"Right good of you, considering he'll be boiled if I catch him. Maybe fried. Kid, would you mind flinging one of those hunks of meat into the oven? Just drop it into a pan, toss some jalapeños over it, turn the oven to four—"

"I know how to put a roast on to cook." She went to the kitchen and washed her hands. When she put jalapeños on the meat, she glanced at the bedroom and tossed a dozen more peppers into the pot. When she finished, she returned to the bedroom.

Jared Calhoun was lying back in bed with his eyes closed and his chest rising and falling evenly. She looked again at his room, the clothes strewn around, the endless books. Beneath the crust there must be a brain, she told herself; he really did know birds. And he was quick. Too quick. There were moments when he seemed so perceptive. She tiptoed around the room gathering up laundry until she spotted a pair of black underwear, the briefest kind. She did not want to touch his underwear. She didn't want to look at it. She dropped a shirt over it, then suddenly had a feeling she was being watched. She looked at the bed, but Jared was breathing as quietly as before. She continued to gather clothing and found another pair of black underwear on top of a pair of dusty hand-tooled boots. Leaving them alone, she glanced again at the bed. He wasn't bad looking when he was asleep. Or when he smiled. It was the in-between times that he seemed so fierce.

She took the clothes to the washer, then tidied up the kitchen for the next hour before returning to the bedroom to check on Jared.

He was sleeping sprawled on the bed, his arms

flung out. He had unbuttoned his shirt. His muscular chest, matted with thick dark curls, rose and fell regularly. She drew a sharp breath as she studied him. He was aggressive even in his sleep. The sight of his body assailed her senses. She couldn't resist one long glance down the length of him, over his slim hips, down the jeans that clung so tightly to muscled legs. She felt a tightening in her loins, a heated longing. What was it about him that made his every touch a burning brand? she asked herself. He had appealing eyes and a teasing smile, but his crusty disposition should erase the good points, only it hadn't. She let her gaze drift slowly upward again, remembering how it felt to be pressed against him.

He was watching her steadily, and she turned fiery red. He sat up, reached for one crutch, and came off the bed in an easy movement. Taking a step backward, she drew a deep breath. He returned her appraisal, his gaze drifting down so slowly, resting on her breasts.

She ached and her lips were tingling, and she wanted to turn around and walk away or say something. Instead, she stood still and watched his eyes rise to hers again. He crossed the room to put his arm around her waist, drawing her to him with a slow, lingering kiss that shut out the world.

The slam of the back door interrupted them.

"Dad, I'm home!"

They moved apart, and Courtney tried to adjust clothing that didn't need straightening. Her face was burning and she wanted to get away.

"Dammit, can you help me?" Jared said.

She put her arm around him to aid him away from the door.

Behind them the door burst open, and a tall, thin boy entered. He had lank brown hair, blue eyes, and a marked resemblance to his father. A blue parka was zipped above faded jeans.

"Dad!" The boy walked in front of them and stopped. "What's the matter with your foot?"

"This is our neighbor, Mrs. Meade. She shot me."

"Tell him what really happened!" Courtney demanded.

"Gee whiz!" Guy blanched and his voice quivered. "Are you gonna be okay?"

"I'm fine. It's nothing serious."

Guy squinted at her, and anger flashed in his eyes. "You Runty Ryan's mom?"

Courtney blinked. "Runty? I'm Ryan Meade's mother."

"Yeah, that's him."

"Be nice, Guy," Jared said.

"Yes, sir." Guy raised his brown eyebrows. "Why? If she shot you."

"I did not shoot your father! Will you tell this child the truth."

"Child? Hell, I'm grown," Guy said in a perfect parody of his father.

"Guy! Don't swear. Apologize," Jared said.

"Sorry," he mumbled, his face flushing.

"If you're so grown, here's your father. You take care of him."

"Hey, wait a minute," Jared said.

"No thanks!" Courtney hurried toward the door, snatching up her coat on the way. She couldn't wait to get out of the house.

She yanked on her jacket as she stepped out the front door into the cold. The sky was still gray and overcast, as dark as her mood. As she walked quickly down the wooden steps Guy Calhoun came running out of the house. "Mrs. Meade, wait!"

She stopped while he jumped off the porch and hurtled toward her. "Here!" he puffed. He jingled a set of silver keys. "Dad said to take the truck. We'll come get it later." He grinned. "Either that or let me drive you home. He said you wouldn't."

"He's right." She took the keys. "Do you really drive?"

He raised his chin and said proudly, "A little on our road. Dad lets me sometimes when we go get the mail."

"Thanks. I'll leave the keys in the truck, and you can come get it."

"Okay. Dad told me you didn't shoot him. He wanted you to know he was teasing. He said it was your fault though. My dad wouldn't shoot himself ever," he added staunchly.

"Well, he did today," she said, but Guy's defense of his father made her anger fade. "Guy, it was an accident," she said gently.

"Yes, ma'am."

She climbed into the red truck and drove away from Jared Calhoun's house trying to calm her frayed nerves.

As she made the last turn in her drive the sight of the single-story house that had been built so long ago smoothed her ruffled emotions. Painted white, the frame house was set high off the ground; its sloping roof sheltered a porch. Sometimes when Courtney turned up the drive, time faded. She almost expected to see her grandmother standing on the porch. Guarding the front door were the two magnolia trees that she had learned at an early age were forbidden to climb. Shaking away the memories, she drove to the back to park beside her Jeep. When she crossed the back porch, she heard a squawk. In a swift dive, Ebeneezer sailed down to land on a windowsill. Courtney dropped some birdseed in front of him.

"You better leave the Calhouns alone," she said. The bird tilted his head to one side. "That's right.

Stay on your own territory or he'll feed you to a great big dog!"

"Who're you talking about, Mom? Who's gonna feed Ebeneezer to a dog?" Ryan held open the kitchen door. He was eating a slice of bread and butter. His blond hair was tousled and his blue corduroy shirttail hung over baggy, loose-fitting jeans.

"Hi, Ryan. I didn't know you were home yet."

"Where'd you get the truck?"

"It belongs to Guy Calhoun's father."

"Guy? How come you're driving it?"

"We had a little altercation today. You're letting cold air into the kitchen." She followed him into the old-fashioned kitchen with glass-fronted cabinets and a round oak table. "I was with a group of bird-watchers, and Mr. Calhoun shot at Ebeneezer."

"Shot at him! Oh, no! He can't do that!"

"He can if Ebeneezer is on his property. Or over his property. He said Ebeneezer scares his horses."

"I'm gonna put Ebeneezer in a cage for a day or two." Ryan pulled on his jacket and headed for the porch.

"That's a good idea."

He opened the back door. "Hey! There's a big white dog here."

"Oh, no! Is Ebeneezer there?"

"Sure is."

Courtney stepped outside and Admiral bounded up to greet her. "Down, Admiral!"

"You know him? Gee, he minds you!"

"He does at that. Too bad Ebeneezer doesn't. Admiral's the Calhouns' dog."

The hawk flew down in front of Admiral's paws. The dog merely wagged his tail. Courtney slipped her fingers beneath Admiral's collar to hold him if he made a lunge.

"One bite, Mom, and old Ebeneezer will be gone."

"I think they like each other. Down, Admiral. Nice dog."

Ryan scratched Admiral's ears, and said, "I'll put Ebeneezer up."

Ryan whistled, and the hawk flew up to perch on Ryan's slender shoulder. He left, walking toward one of the large cages they used occasionally for injured birds.

Courtney knelt down to pat Admiral, running her hands through his thick coat while his tail thumped. She watched her son, a small boy with a red-tailed hawk perched on his shoulder, and heard Guy Calhoun's derisive taunt, "Runty." Was that what he called Ryan at school? Was school difficult for Ryan? Guy was the newcomer, but sometimes that didn't make any difference. She stood up and looked down at Admiral. "At least Ryan isn't growing up on soda pop!"

Admiral's tail thumped vigorously.

"You're entirely too nice for that household. I know why you followed me home."

Admiral wagged his tail happily. "Unfortunately, I have to report your presence, and they'll take you when they come for the truck."

Another wag. She leaned down to scratch his ears. "You're a nice dog, Admiral. Too bad your master can't take lessons." Idly, she ran her fingers through the white fur and gazed into space, speaking softly. "I guess that wasn't fair. Your master has his moments when he isn't half bad. Ummm, not bad at all . . ." Her voice trailed away, her thoughts swirling with impressions of Jared, his crustiness and his sensitivity. His knowledge of birds and his determination to shoot Ebeneezer.

She tilted the dog's face up and gazed into the happy eyes. "I'll never understand men, Admiral. Never."

He thumped his tail. Shaking her head, she stood up and went inside. Throughout the evening, when she tried to forget Jared Calhoun, she succeeded for whole minutes at a time—until bedtime. That night she lay in bed staring into the darkness, remembering in detail Jared Calhoun's kisses, the twinkle in his eyes, and his deep voice.

She groaned and rolled over, squeezing her eyes shut, trying to forget, but it wasn't until the early morning that she fell asleep to dream of a red-tailed hawk flying over a tall man with blue, blue eyes.

The next day when she went into the kitchen, the red truck was gone. She spent the day painting signs with information for visitors to the sanctuary—and trying not to wonder how Jared was getting on alone. At half-past four Ryan arrived home.

As he came up the driveway from the road she glanced out the kitchen window and her heart turned over. Her son's nose was bleeding, his eye was turning dark, and his lip was puffed. His coat was torn and covered with dirt.

Five

"Ryan!" She ran outside into the misty air, shivering in spite of her flannel shirt and jeans. "Ryan, what on earth happened? Did you fall off the bus?"

He squinted up at her and wiped his nose with the back of his hand, then glanced down at his bloody hand. She could see where tears had streaked his cheeks.

"What happened?"

"I was in a fight, Mom. I'm all right."

"Oh, Ryan!" Her knees began to shake. Feeling totally inadequate to cope with the problem, she wanted to pull him to her and hold him tightly, but she squared her shoulders determinedly. "Honey, come in and I'll help you clean up. Do any bones feel broken? Maybe we better go into town—"

"Mom, I'm gonna live. I just had a fight." He sniffed, and she saw his eyes fill with tears.

"Who did it?"

"Guy Calhoun. He said you hurt his dad!

Because of you his dad was shot. I know you don't own a gun. You don't even know how to load a gun!"

"Ohhh!" Fear, anguish, and torment funneled together, boiling into rage. "Guy Calhoun."

Ryan gazed up at her. "You're mad, huh? If I had a dad, he'd go punch Old Man Calhoun, wouldn't he, Mom?"

"Oh, heavens, Ryan!" She fought back tears that struck without warning. "Come on, honey, let me help you."

They went into the bathroom, and Courtney struggled with faintness as she worked on her son. She dabbed at his injuries with the washcloth, muttering under her breath, trembling because she couldn't bear to see anyone or anything injured, far worse, to see her son hurt. "Are your teeth okay?"

"I dunno. One's kinda loose."

"Show me." She watched him wiggle a tooth.

"I'll call the dentist." She felt icy, shivering and trying to keep her teeth from chattering until she got him cleaned up. When she touched his cheek he yelled.

"Ouch!" Tears brimmed over and fell down his cheeks. "I hate Guy Calhoun!"

"Don't hate."

"I do. He's a bully!"

"Ryan, when did he do this?"

"When we got off the bus."

"Here, honey. Just a little more and I'm through."

"He said he'd beat me up again tomorrow if I don't admit you hurt his dad."

"Oh! No, he won't. I can meet the bus."

"No."

"No? You just said he's a bully. He's almost as tall as I am."

"No. Don't meet the bus, Mom. I have to be a man."

"Oh, Ryan." She put her arms around him and hugged his frail body to her, trying to keep the tears back. "Ryan, I want to meet you at the bus stop."

"No, Mom. Please, don't. Promise me you won't."

She leaned back to look into eyes filled with misery. "You're sure?"

"I'm sure."

She finished with cleaning his cuts. "What would you like to eat most of all?"

"I don't feel like chewing. Can we have fried chicken? And mashed potatoes and biscuits?"

She smiled down at him, a surge of relief coursing through her. "I can tell you don't feel like chewing. You do your homework while I get dinner."

Two hours later as Ryan lay before his books spread out on the living room floor, Courtney pulled on her coat.

"Honey, get your coat. I want you to come with me while I run an errand."

"Where're you going?"

"I'm going to see 'Old Man Calhoun.' "

Ryan's eyes became round. "You are? For me?"

"Yes."

"You can't punch him out."

"No, but I can tell him a thing or two."

"Gee whiz!" Ryan scrambled up, pulling on his jacket as he followed her to the door. He sounded awestruck. "You really gonna do that?"

"I have a few words to say about this to Mr. Calhoun and his son."

She opened the door and saw a flash of white, then Admiral jumped up.

"You again. Come on, you go home now."

"He likes us better'n them, Mom."

"I know. Can't blame him." She climbed into her Jeep, whistled for Admiral, and turned the key. The ignition ground loudly, then died. She tried again. On the fourth attempt it caught, and she shifted gears and headed for the road. It was a cold, misty night; she wanted to be home. As she thought about Jared's attitude and Guy Calhoun's threats, she wanted to wring two necks! Her temper rose and was churning and boiling by the time she stopped in front of the Calhouns' house.

"I won't be a minute, Ryan," she said as she opened her door. "Just wait here, please."

"Yes, ma'am."

She stomped to the front door and pushed the bell while Admiral stood at her knees and wagged his tail.

When the door opened, Guy faced her. His face flushed as he drew a deep breath. "Oh, Mrs. Meade!"

"Is your father home?"

"Yes, ma'am, but he doesn't feel good."

"Who is it, Guy?" a deep voice said.

"Mrs. Meade."

"Tell her to come in."

Reluctantly, Guy stepped back. "Mrs. Meade, are you—" He clamped his lips closed and moved out of the way. "He's in the front room."

Courtney went inside and saw Jared seated in a large leather chair. His blue shirt was open at the throat and his dark hair glinted softly in the light. His bandaged foot was propped up before him. She crossed the room swiftly and faced him.

"Well, to what do I owe this pleasant surprise?" he asked. "You going to shoot me in the other foot?" He laughed, then pushed himself up, put his crutches under his arms, and stood up.

She clenched her fists. "Your son has a false idea

of what happened yesterday. You need to set him straight."

"You hurt my dad!"

"Guy!" Jared snapped. "What the hell is all this about?"

Her voice calmed. "Guy, would you like to tell your father?"

"It was nothin', Dad." He shifted his feet and studied his shoes.

"Guy," Jared said sternly.

"I was in a fight with Ryan Meade," he said so softly he was barely audible.

"Why?"

"Because his mom shot you."

"Guy, I told you clearly what really happened." Jared's voice was harsh.

"You wouldn't shoot yourself!" Guy's face was flushed, and he looked anguished, softening Courtney's anger.

"You wait in your room and we'll discuss it!" Jared said.

"Gee, Dad, I did it because—" He bit off his words, flinching beneath Jared's scowl.

Suddenly Courtney realized Guy was as vulnerable as Ryan. He wanted his father's approval so badly; perhaps the reasons for the fight ran deep.

"Because of what?" Jared's clipped words made Guy chew his lip.

While the uncomfortable silence lengthened, Courtney asked gently, "You did it for your father, didn't you?"

Guy's eyes widened, then filled with tears. He turned and ran out of the room.

Jared ran his fingers through his hair, the short dark brown waves springing away. "I think you saw something there I didn't," he said, sounding uncertain. "I don't know why he'd fight with your son. I told him it was an accident."

"Maybe he's frightened that you were hurt. He might be afraid of losing you too."

Jared swore softly, staring at the empty doorway through which his son had gone.

"Damn. I try so hard to think how Leah would be with him if she were here. I'm doing the best I can, but there are times when my best just isn't enough."

"I know how you feel. I can't be a father to Ryan. All I can do is love him."

"My father didn't give a damn about my brothers and me. I can't bear for Guy to feel that I don't care. At the same time, I don't want to spoil him rotten. Sometimes I feel so damned helpless." Again his fingers raked through his hair.

"No one is perfect. You know that. Love will have to make up for mistakes." Suddenly, she saw a side to Jared Calhoun that she wouldn't have guessed possible. He seemed unsure, so much a single parent with all the responsibilities and cares it meant. She knew full well what he was going through.

"Why don't you sit down," he said suddenly. "We'll talk about it."

"No, Ryan's out in the jeep waiting, and it's cold. You and your son can talk about it. He's threatened Ryan."

"Threatened?"

"Yes. He threatened to beat him up after school tomorrow."

"Oh, damn," Jared said tiredly. His voice hardened, and he said, "He won't. You can set your mind at ease." His brows came together, giving him a fierce expression that stirred in Courtney a deeper trace of sympathy for Guy.

"I brought your dog home," she said. "For some reason, he has decided to hang around our house."

"Tell you what," Jared said thoughtfully, "let's

have a little talk about the boys. Come over for lunch tomorrow."

"I don't see any need for that, and you can't stand up to cook."

"Come while the boys are at school and let's discuss this. I'd like a woman's opinions." His frown vanished. "You can do the cooking."

Suddenly she felt at a loss. She wondered if she should agree, because they could talk freely.

"All right," she said. "Noon. I'll bring lunch."

"Good."

She left then. In the jeep she held her breath when it merely made a clicking noise at the turn of the ignition, but finally it caught and she drove away with Ryan watching her closely.

"What happened, Mom?"

"You won't have to worry about Guy tomorrow."

"How come?"

"His father promised he'd handle Guy. I think Mr. Calhoun was very angry, Ryan."

"Oh." He settled in the seat, a frown on his brow while he thought about it. She remembered Guy's face blanching, his attention on his father.

"Mr. Calhoun is kinda scary," Ryan said.

"You know him?"

"He was at school once. He's sorta gruff."

"He is at that."

"I think I'd rather have a fight with Guy than have Mr. Calhoun mad at me." He looked up at her. "You're pretty brave, Mom."

"Why thank you!" She accepted the compliment with warmth, glancing at Ryan. "Mr. Calhoun wants me to come over tomorrow and discuss it more."

"He does? Will you go?"

"I don't know if it'll help."

"It might. You always tell me to try to work things out."

"I guess so." She smiled at him. "I said I'd go, and I will."

"I'm getting hungry."

"Want milk and cookies?" she asked, realizing the issue was closed in Ryan's mind.

The next morning she kissed Ryan good-bye and said a small prayer that he would get home safely. She set about preparing lunch, and the more she worked and thought about her dealings with Jared Calhoun, the more agitated she became. Worry over Ryan and Guy was compounded by the threat to Ebeneezer. She also wished she didn't have such a definite reaction to Jared, and beneath it all lay a kernel of anger over his continual use of "kid" to address her.

She thought about her appearance. With one long pigtail down her back, no makeup, and wearing jeans, she could see why he called her kid. He wasn't the first person to misjudge her age by years.

Well, maybe at lunch she would end that! She went upstairs, drew a bath of hot water, and began to lay out her clothes.

By noon, she was ready. She stopped to take inventory. She was wearing jeans and a blue sweater, nothing too feminine there, but her hair hung to her waist in shimmering waves of gold. She wore a slight touch of lipstick and blush, her lashes had been brushed lightly with mascara, and a faint aura of perfume surrounded her. She carried the lunch out to the Jeep in a picnic basket and then struggled to get the vehicle started and drove off.

Six

Courtney knocked and heard Jared's cheerful call to come in. When she entered, he was standing in the hallway waiting.

"Golly, gee whiz, as you'd say," he said. "I'm impressed."

She blushed and felt a rush of pleasure along with a jolting awareness of his appearance. He was leaning with one hip against the doorjamb, and his jeans pulled tautly across his hips, and the brown hand-tooled belt angled down slightly. The sleeves of his brown sweater were pushed above his elbows, revealing muscular forearms sprinkled with short dark hair. The sweater, the jeans, fit snugly and revealed the wiry fitness of the body beneath them. *The body beneath them.* Her heart lurched at the thought.

"Thank you," she said. "Where shall I put lunch?"

"Who cares?"

"What?"

He grinned. "Oh, yeah, kid. Lunch. In the kitchen." He followed her into the kitchen and sat down in a chair, propping his injured foot on another one.

She set the basket down, then turned and caught him examining her. When his gaze lifted from her hips to her breasts and paused, she wished she hadn't chosen a sweater. Through the thin lace bra and the soft woolen sweater, his glance touched like a warm caress. Her breasts became tight and she drew a deep breath, wondering if she would ever learn. Air filled her lungs, and her breasts thrust against the material.

"Mr. Calhoun, are you ready to eat?"

He arched one brow, raised his eyes to hers, and drawled the most suggestive double entendre she had ever heard. "Oh, yeah, I'm ready, kid."

Several things happened at once. Her system reacted to his sensuous voice like a hot tin roof zapped by rain. She sizzled. Her psyche suffered because he still called her kid, and her mind fumed because he got to her effortlessly, instantly, and totally. With the arch of a brow, a few words, a leer, he could change her pulse, her mind, her breathing. She wanted to slam shut the picnic basket and go home. She thought of her son's bloody, bruised face and gritted her teeth.

"Now you're angry," Jared said. "You're a touchy sort, kid, you know?"

"I promised my son I'd come see 'Old Man Calhoun' today."

His straight white teeth showed in a broad smile. "That's me. Sounds as if your son has a little pizzazz."

"He has plenty of pizzazz, but he's little and he doesn't have a father to help him in a crisis such as the one your son caused."

"There won't be another one. I made that clear to Guy. And if you'll send Ryan over here, I'll teach him to defend himself."

"That's the last thing I want! I don't want him to learn to box. I want your son to stop. You've allowed Guy to harbor a misconception. I didn't shoot you, and you know it!"

"You were the definite cause. First gun accident I've had in my life, and I've had a gun since I was eight years old."

"That figures. Did you tell him I didn't shoot you?"

"Smooth your feathers down. I have."

"And then, in the same breath, added that I caused it."

"Only the truth. But I explained you did it to save a hawk."

She thought about Guy's swearing the first time they met, sounding so like his father, his defensive attitude about his dad, and his need for Jared's approval. "I think your son adores you," she said.

Jared's face flushed, but his eyes sparkled, revealing his pleasure. "We get along pretty well, but sometimes I wonder if I'm handling things right."

"I know what you mean. I offered to meet the bus today, and Ryan wouldn't have any part of it. He said he had to be a man."

"Good for him. He'll get along. Guy has a short fuse, but he won't pick a fight today. We went over that thoroughly."

While he talked, Courtney realized they were having a discussion about their sons, and it was nice.

"Let's see what the basket holds," he said.

"What do you want to drink? A beer?"

"Sure enough, kid."

"How's your foot today?"

"Hurts worse than before. Maybe the shock is wearing off. Maybe it was your kisses that kept my mind off it."

To hide her blush and the peculiar pleasure she felt, she muttered, "I can imagine how long since the last time you kissed a woman."

He chuckled.

As if on cue, the phone beside her rang. He nodded to her to answer it, and she picked it up and said hello.

"Jared?" a woman's voice said.

"Just a minute, please." She handed the phone to Jared. "Sounds like your mother." He grinned. Courtney knew it wasn't his mother, and while she unloaded the basket, she couldn't help listening to the conversation.

"Hi, Trudy," he said. "A neighbor's here. We're having lunch and talking about P.T.A., that sort of thing. P.T.A.—pretty, tall, and available."

Courtney knocked over an empty glass. She heard his chuckle and a shriek from the phone that would rival Ebeneezer's, then Jared said, "Just kidding, Trudy. It's Parent-Teacher Association. We have sons in the same school."

Silence. And anger. Courtney picked up the glass and filled it.

"I'll call you later, hon," Jared said, his voice lowered a fraction.

Hon. Courtney's temperature jumped. He called some woman hon, while he had addressed her only as kid, including today, when her hair was clean and falling free, her clothes were attractive, and she wore a touch of makeup. It made no difference what Mr. Jared Calhoun did, she told herself. But it did. She glanced at him. He was relaxed, telephone in hand, his blue eyes on her. Why was it important what he did? Why was there a slight sting when he called another woman hon? Was it a purely feminine response, or something deeper?

He hung up. "Did you drop something?"

"I picked it up." She poured a cola for herself, then carried it and his beer to the table. When she set them down, he grasped her wrist and pulled her onto his lap. He did it so quickly, he caught her off guard. She started to spring up, but his arm slipped around her waist and held her.

"Sit still. You'll hurt my foot if you wiggle."

"I bet," she answered, barely aware of what she said. He smelled nice, he was clean-shaven, and his gaze was so intense.

He touched her hair. "Your hair's pretty."

"Thank you, Mr. Calhoun."

"Jared. We're way beyond Mr. and Mrs., kid."

"We're not to the lap-sitting stage, though."

He touched strands of her hair to his cheek while he studied every inch of her features. "Don't know why not. I like this. And if you were half-honest and one-tenth less prudish, you'd admit you like it too."

"You have all the charm of a cocklebur," she said, but her breathless voice tempered the accusation.

He grinned. "Do tell, kid. A cocklebur!" He chuckled.

She tried to get up, but there wasn't anywhere to put her hands. She could feel his knees beneath her and she was entirely too close to a mouth that had no similarity whatsoever to a cocklebur. Lips that were slightly full, well defined, and sensual. Oh, so sensual!

"Your arm won't burn off if you put your hand on my shoulder," he said.

"Will you let me up?"

"Don't see any reason to. Relax. Talk about cock-leburs! You do act like you're sitting on one." He let her long, silky hair slide through his fingers. "Like gold."

"What is?"

"You know damn well."

She blushed, firmed her lips, and started to get up, but his arm tightened, and she was held.

"What you need is to be kissed soundly, then you'd stop all this antsy urge to run."

"You take the prize for cantankerous, ornery creatures!" She tried to sound forceful, to ignore the blaze kindling inside her.

"And you, kid, are spunky, teasable, and too tempting to resist. Close your eyes."

"No-o-o . . ."

"Courtney, I want to kiss you," he said softly, solemnly.

Her protest vanished along with his teasing. She wanted him to kiss her, and he must have seen it in her expression. He pulled her close, taking possession of her mouth. Wrapping his arms around her, he cradled her against his shoulder. She slipped an arm around his neck and felt his soft, wavy hair touch the back of her hand. She lost awareness of everything except his kiss. He settled down to the business of kissing with an enthusiasm that made her heart skip beats. Her system forgot Mr. Calhoun was a cocklebur. He became a sexy, sensual man who could tease and stroke her to a melting softness.

She clung to him, surrendering to the languorous kiss. His hand trailed around her narrow waist, then moved upward, seeking her breast. Pressed against him, she could feel his arousal. Caution returned with the force of a tidal wave. She pushed away.

"That's enough," she said.

He gazed at her with a smoldering hunger that almost made her fling her arms around him again.

"It's not anywhere near enough," he said huskily. He caught strands of her hair again, toying with them. "What happened, kid? Bad marriage make you so touchy?"

"No, and I'd rather not discuss what makes me tick," she said hurriedly, trying to catch her breath. Then she changed her mind. "You always want to know why I'm so prudish. It doesn't have anything to do with my marriage. It's just ingrained in me. I grew up in a house full of delicate southern ladies who were always prim and proper and raised me to be that way."

"What about your father?" he asked gently.

"He was as refined and dignified as the women in the family. And I barely remember a time when he wasn't ill. He was frail and quiet and loved to read. I had it drummed into my head from the time I could toddle that I should act like a little lady, that I should be neat, circumspect, and correct."

"No kidding?"

"Absolute truth. Disorder makes me nervous."

"No wonder it's only on the surface." His voice lowered. "I think deep inside you is a woman who's more loving and a little wild than she is proper and correct."

"I hope so." She sighed. "And maybe deep inside you is a man who isn't half so stormy and crusty."

His eyes twinkled momentarily. "Deep down, I'm just a pure lovable softy."

"Why do I have doubts?" She smiled, gazing into his blue eyes to discover a speculative look that burned like a banked campfire. She quickly slipped off his lap and walked to the counter, aware of his amusement as she did.

She set everything on the table. She had brought tuna fish sandwiches, potato chips, a bowl of potato salad, and deviled eggs. "That's quite a spread," he remarked.

"I thought you might like a change."

"Hmmm. What's between the bread?"

"Tuna fish."

He winced. She frowned at him. "You don't like tuna fish?"

"I can't wait to try it."

"You don't like it!"

"Kid, anything you fix, I'll eat, even if it's plastic between two slabs of rock."

"You don't have to eat my tuna sandwiches."

"Sit down. Quit fussing and dithering around."

She tightened her lips and sat down, hoping he choked on the tuna. As he took a healthy helping of potato salad, he asked, "Do you mind getting some pepper sauce?"

"Not at all."

"Golly, gee whillikers. If words could freeze, you wouldn't have to use electricity to cool things down."

She set the pepper sauce on the table, sat down, and shook her head when he offered her peppers. She watched with mild horror as he opened his sandwich and stacked a generous helping of hot peppers over her tuna fish, then sprinkled pepper sauce on it. He glanced up. "Sure you don't want some?"

"Why don't you just eat bread and peppers?"

"I'm glad to try your tuna. Kid, when I think about you going to all this trouble for me, I'm flattered."

She blushed and wished she hadn't brought lunch. "I'd do the same for any—"

"Don't say it. Let me have the pleasure of thinking you slaved over tuna fish and potatoes all morning just for me," he said, sounding so sincere she stared at him. When her gaze lowered to his sandwich, she shuddered. "It's a wonder you haven't burned your stomach away."

"I've still got one." His eyes crinkled. "Want me to show you?"

"No!"

He chuckled and touched her jaw. "You lead with your chin, kid."

She wondered why she had agreed to subject herself to another hour of his company. As quickly as the question rose to mind, she thought of their pleasant discussion of the boys. She had to admit, there were moments when he was just plain enjoyable in spite of his teasing. Moments. She thought of his kisses and blushed hotly.

"Now what on earth is on your mind?" he asked.

"Nothing."

"Oh, my. You turn as red as a Holland tulip, then say 'nothing.' That sounds really good! I hope I'm included."

She knew her blush deepened. She tried to be cool and face him.

"What was your husband like?" he asked suddenly.

She looked out the window, seeing Mason's brown eyes, remembering the way they darkened when he was angry. The last thing she would discuss with Jared Calhoun was Mason Meade. "That was a long time ago. What was your wife like?"

"You can't imagine, can you?" The teasing note was back in his voice.

"It's difficult. Mind-boggling, as a matter of fact. There's a woman in your life now."

He paused before taking a bite and shook his head. "Trudy? Secretary. She works for me."

"You work? I thought this farm was your business."

"I have an office in town, but I don't go any more often than I have to. I'm closing it. It was a commercial real estate office I had with my wife. My heart hasn't been in it. I'm winding up the last of it now. I want to settle down to a little farming, to raising my horses, and taking care of Guy. Years have a way of slipping past before you know it."

They ate quietly then. When they were finished, he reached across the table to touch her hand. "Kid," he said while he trailed his fingers across her knuckles, tracing the shape of each of her slender fingers, creating tingles that distracted her attention, "I don't think Guy will lay a hand on your son again, but if he does, let me know right away."

"You weren't too harsh, were you?"

He frowned. "No. It doesn't take much to bring Guy around to reason. You ought to let Ryan learn how to defend himself though."

"I don't want Ryan to learn how to fight." She sounded breathless and wanted to yank her hand out of his reach, but she couldn't move. "Ryan is small, and he doesn't know anything about fighting." She slipped her hand away, and her voice steadied. "And that's the way it should be. I'm not raising a hooligan who thinks issues can be settled by fists."

"Oh, damn, kid, that's no way to raise a boy. Let the child know how to defend himself."

"Everything you do is physical," she said, and the conversation took another turn.

He tilted his chair back, hooked his thumbs in his belt, and studied her intently. "There are a lot of fun things that are physical," he said softly.

She drew a deep breath and began to wonder if she could spend five minutes in the presence of Jared Calhoun without blushing. "Don't change the subject!"

"I didn't. I'm pursuing your remark."

"We were talking about our boys. And I can see I'm getting nowhere now. Your head is as hard as the rest of you."

He grinned. "I could say something to bring the pink back to your cheeks, but I won't."

Her temper was rising. She stood up, picked up the lunch things, and began to clean.

"Just leave them," Jared said. "Guy'll do the dishes when he gets home."

"I can imagine."

"He did the breakfast dishes."

She turned around to ask, "What was your wife like? Did she eat hot peppers and drink beer and swear?"

"Leah was nice. Mighty nice. And there isn't anything wrong with a woman or man eating hot peppers, drinking beer, or swearing. Kid, you have a prudish streak a mile wide." He smiled. "Until you kiss. Thank heaven. You lose it then."

She turned back around and continued cleaning off the counter.

"Just leave that alone. When I woke up yesterday, I couldn't find half my clothes."

"I washed them."

"You didn't wash my underwear."

She felt an urge to swear. "Oh, didn't I?"

"You know damn well you didn't. You neatly covered them up with my shirt and left them. Your husband have to wash his underwear for you?"

"I'm going home." She quickly started gathering up her things.

"I just asked if—"

"Mr. Calhoun, you're an ornery, oversexed cocklebur!"

He grinned and tilted his chair back farther, bending his good leg. "An oversexed cocklebur! You like to kiss. No matter how much you huff and puff and blow about it, kid, you like it!" She blushed furiously and worked faster.

"If you get any speedier, you're gonna blow a fuse."

She shot him a look that didn't faze him.

"When the school carnival comes, I'll pick you up and the four of us can go together."

"Thank you, no! Are you taking peppers and beer?"

"Might take some peppers. The boys could get to know each other."

"Thanks, but Ryan and Guy know each other well enough now. And neither can stand the other."

"Might change if given half a chance."

"They're definitely not the same type."

"That's okay. You and I aren't the same type, but we fit together."

Startled, she frowned. "How can you say that?"

"We can talk about birds or boys." His blue eyes twinkled. "We can—"

"Never mind! I'm not sure I want to hear," she said, but she was smiling, and he grinned. "How come you know so much about birds?"

"With one exception of course, I like birds. I like horses, boys, the outdoors. Leah belonged to the Audubon Society for a few years. I used to go with her. Matter-of-fact, I just acquired two pairs of swans for the pond."

"You did? Oh, how nice! They're so pretty."

"I think so too. Since the pond is on both properties, you'll probably see them. See, we can agree. And not only can I identify feathery critters, I had a pet crow once."

"And you're going to shoot Ryan's hawk?"

"That's another kettle of fish. A bird of a different feather might be a better way to say it. He's mean as sin."

"Ebeneezer is a pet. A tame hawk who wouldn't intentionally hurt anyone or anything."

"Not so, kid."

The sound of a motor interrupted them, growing

louder as a car approached. Jared tipped back his chair again to gaze out the window.

"Here comes my brother Kent."

"How many brothers do you have?"

"Two. Lonnie and Kent."

The motor sputtered into silence, a door slammed, and boots clattered across the porch. Immediately after knocking, Kent opened the door and thrust his head inside. "Jared! Oh, there you are."

"Come in, Kent. Meet my neighbor, Mrs. Courtney Meade. Courtney, this is Kent Calhoun."

"Hey, there," he greeted her, and stepped into the kitchen. His wavy brown hair and blue eyes resembled Jared's, but Kent had a broader face and was a few inches shorter than his brother. Within minutes Courtney realized the similarities between them were purely physical. Kent said, "I've got car trouble. Thought you might be able to fix it. What happened to your foot?"

Courtney braced herself for another onslaught, but instead, listened with amazement as Jared said, "I had an accident with my gun."

"You shot yourself in the foot?" Kent's eyes widened in surprise.

"I caused it," Courtney said. If Jared could be nice enough to admit the truth, she could too. "I jumped over the fence and tripped and bumped into him, making his gun discharge."

Jared winked at her as if in acknowledgment that they could be civilized over the accident.

"Is it bad?" Kent asked.

"Naw. It's superficial. Hurts like hell, but no permanent damage."

"Feel like checking my car?"

"Yep. If you'll excuse us, Courtney." Jared rose, steadied himself with the crutch, and hobbled to the door. After pulling on his jacket, he and Kent went outside. She watched through the window while Jared raised the hood and bent over the engine.

Within minutes Kent returned. "I need to take him a toolbox." He opened the kitchen closet. "Shucks, it isn't in here." He stepped out of the closet and scratched his head.

"Can I help you?" Courtney asked.

"Yeah. Jared's not the soul of neatness. No telling where it is. It's a green metal box like a tackle box. You search the living room, and I'll poke through his bedroom."

As they walked across the kitchen, she said, "You're not as gruff as your brother."

"Jared? I guess he seems gruff. I'm so used to his swearing and all, I don't think about it. He comes by it naturally, because he bore the brunt of Dad's anger. He was a buffer between our dad and Lonnie and me. That box could be anywhere. Under the sofa, on a bookshelf."

"I'll look around," she said, but her thoughts were on what Kent had just revealed about Jared. A buffer between his father and younger brothers. Kent had said it so casually, as if thoroughly accustomed to the arrangement. A buffer against what? she wondered. Parental strictness, or was it something deeper—anger and hostility? She hunted through papers and magazines while Kent searched in the bedroom. Within a few minutes he reappeared.

"*Ta da!* I found it!" He held up the box.

"Good." As they fell into step together on their way to the kitchen he glanced at her.

"You married?"

"Divorced. I have a son the same age as Guy."

"Oh."

She was aware of a closer scrutiny, and suddenly she wanted some answers about Mr. Jared

Calhoun. With an uncustomary bluntness, she asked, "You said Jared bore the brunt of your dad's anger. Was your father cruel?"

Kent paused at the door; his blue eyes went flat and cold. "Our dad was meaner than a snake. Jared took a lot of lumps for me. Actually, Jared's the only dad I claim." The harshness vanished as Kent smiled. "Don't let Jared scare you. He just seems gruff. Beneath the surface he's peaches and cream. Soft as mush."

"Yeah, sure."

Kent laughed and slammed the door behind him. Courtney moved to the window to watch while Jared rummaged through the green toolbox, removed a wrench, propped his bad foot on the bumper, and bent over the engine again. While Jared worked, Kent stood with his thumbs hooked into his belt, watching Jared and talking.

Kent's words rattled around in her thoughts. "He's peaches and cream." That was stretching it a bit! "Meaner than a snake." How cold the words had sounded. So terribly harsh. "He bore the brunt . . . the only dad I claim."

Jared straightened, putting his weight on the crutch while Kent climbed behind the wheel and started the engine. Once again, Jared bent over it. Courtney sat down where she could watch them. Finally Jared slammed the hood down, wiped his hands on a rag from the toolbox, and talked a moment to Kent who had stepped out of the car again. Jared reached into his hip pocket, pulled out his billfold, and gave some bills to Kent, then watched as Kent climbed into the car and drove off.

Jared picked up the toolbox carefully. He turned and limped back to the house, swinging the crutch when his weight was on his good foot, carrying the toolbox to the porch.

After washing his hands at the kitchen sink, he

sat down across from her. "Now Kent's car will run for a few more weeks."

"I take it you don't have to comb his hair or wash his face," Courtney said.

Jared chuckled and shrugged. "Habit dies hard."

"How old is he?"

"He's the youngest. Twenty-five."

"Is the other one as dependent on you?"

"Lonnie? Not quite."

"Who takes care of you?"

"Me, myself, and I. I was the oldest in a house of men. My mother died when Kent was born. I think Dad blamed us for all his troubles. If you think I'm gruff, you should've known him. He had a high temper and couldn't hold a job long."

The same flat tone that had been in Kent's voice had crept into Jared's, and it was just as chilling. "Dad's dead now."

"I'm sorry."

He shrugged. "Kent's engaged, Lonnie's married and has three little boys." He laughed. "Talk about fights! Lonnie's boys are live wires. They live in Nashville."

"What kind of work do your brothers do?"

"Kent has a landscaping business. Lonnie is a dentist. I get my teeth fixed." He flashed a white smile, looking as if he seldom needed his brother's services. "I keep their books for them. I think I'm raising Guy to be more independent than my brothers."

"Maybe that's why." She paused. "It's getting late."

"I can't get out to my horses. It'll be a long afternoon. Don't rush off."

"I came over to discuss the boys. We have, and I need to go home. A group of sixth graders are coming in an hour."

"Come sit in my lap and kiss me good-bye before you go."

"Like h—" She stopped short, shocked at what she had started to say. He laughed and wagged his finger at her.

"What happened to, 'Oh, drat!'?"

"I've been around you too much." She stood up.

"Get the potato salad out of the fridge. You forgot it."

She crossed the room and opened the refrigerator. She took out the potato salad, slammed the door, and turned, almost colliding against Jared Calhoun. He was leaning on one crutch. His free arm went over her shoulder, and his hand brushed the back of her neck.

Courtney tried to ignore the flurry of tingles that followed his touch.

"Seems a waste of a good afternoon for you to go," he said.

"It isn't. Will you move out of the way? I'd hate to push over a man on crutches," she said, while she felt heat rush up in waves.

"Hate for you to." His voice lowered, his thumb ran back and forth across the nape of her neck, stirring fiery currents.

"Move out of the way, please, Mr. Calhoun."

"Sounds as if the wind has gone out of your sails, kid."

"There are actually moments," she said softly, "when I think all your unpleasant ways are only skin deep. That's what Kent said too."

He brushed her ear lightly, tracing his finger over the curve of it, sending delicious tickles throughout her. "And there are moments when I think your prudishness is just skin deep. Jared," he said huskily, coaxingly. "Let me hear you say it."

"You're really exasperating," she said, but her

voice had become a breathless whisper. "Am I going to have to fight you off?"

He smiled briefly, then sobered. "No, you don't have to fight me off, but I want to hear you say Jared."

She glared at him while her heartbeat drummed. "Jared. There. I said it, now you keep your part of the bargain and move out of my way."

He did and she went home, her thoughts in a turmoil over his actions and her response. Jared Calhoun was a confusing combination of friendliness and gruffness, of teasing banter and sexy kisses. She considered his brother, Kent. When he had discovered Jared's injury, he hadn't asked if he could stay or help. Instead, he had asked Jared for help. "He was a buffer between our dad for Lonnie and me." Perhaps Jared had a good reason for his manner. Something in their past had to have been bad for both men to get that glacial chill in their voices when they spoke of their father.

During the afternoon while she followed the winding trail through the sanctuary, pointing out to the sixth graders the nesting places of various birds or waiting until a bird was sighted, she found it difficult to get Jared out of her thoughts.

Ryan came home his usual cheerful self. Nothing was said about Guy Calhoun. While she began writing a report for one of her courses, Ryan spread out his school books beside her at the kitchen table. They hadn't been working more than fifteen minutes when Courtney heard a car motor. She glanced out the window to see the Calhouns' pickup slowing to a halt by her Jeep. Jared and Guy, who was red-faced and gloomy, climbed down.

"Who is it, Mom?" Ryan asked.

"I'd guess from the expression on Guy Calhoun's face, his father is making him apologize to you."

"Gee whiz! You're kiddin'!" Ryan peeped out the window, his brows rising. "Boy! I'd hate that."

"It's probably twice as hard for Guy as it would be for you." She opened the back door and crossed the porch to meet them.

Jared stopped, folded his arms across his chest, and waited. Guy glanced at his father, then stepped forward as reluctantly as if he were going to run a gauntlet.

"Mrs. Meade, is Ryan here?"

"Yes."

"Hi," Ryan said, suddenly appearing beside her.

"I'm sorry for the things I said about your mother," Guy mumbled in a rush, his cheeks matching his red eyes. The instant he apologized, his gaze slid to his dad, and some silent exchange seemed to take place as Jared nodded. Courtney realized how difficult it had been to apologize and that Guy desperately wanted Jared's approval. There was no belligerence or resentment in his expression, merely a hunger for approval, which Jared gave instantly.

"That's okay," Ryan answered solemnly, and an uncomfortable silence descended.

"Thank you, Guy," Courtney said softly, feeling sorry for the boy in spite of what he'd done. "Ryan, why don't you show Guy the injured mallard we found today."

"Okay. I'll get my coat." He did, and the two boys walked down the path toward the cages. Courtney faced Jared.

"Thanks," she said. "I know that was hard for both of you."

"Yeah, but necessary. I think Guy learned his lesson."

"Want to come in? I can make some hot chocolate."

"Sure."

He followed her inside, pausing to gaze around. He seemed to fill the kitchen as he pulled off his sheepskin jacket and settled in a chair to watch her.

"Guy wants your approval badly," she said.

"It's been that way since Leah's death. He wasn't that way before. I figured maybe Leah gave him something I can't."

"Well, she probably did. Children don't get the exact same thing from each parent, but you gave him approval before, didn't you?"

"Damn right," Jared said bitterly. "I love Guy and I intend that he knows it."

"Unlike your father."

"Yeah."

"Don't worry." Courtney placed a pan on the stove and reached for the milk. "If you love Guy and give him approval, you're probably doing fine."

"I hope so. This kind of threw me."

While she stirred the milk, watching the swirls in the white liquid, Jared propped his injured foot on another chair and leaned back. He picked up a book and studied the cover. *"Bird Migration,"* he read aloud. "Is this one of your textbooks?"

"Yes, I sometimes do my homework when Ryan does his. I'm here to help him if he has a question."

Jared put the book down. "Since Leah's been gone, Guy's done some goofy things. Like there's some anger down deep inside—" He broke off as a clatter on the porch interrupted him and Guy appeared.

"Dad, come with me and see the birds they have. Their hawk, Ebeneezer, perched on my shoulder. Ryan taught me how to whistle to him. Let me show you."

Jared pulled on his jacket and adjusted the crutch beneath his arm. "Sure. Mrs. Meade's fixing hot chocolate."

"Do you like hot chocolate, Guy?"

"Yes, ma'am. Dad, they have a duck that has an injured wing, but it lets Ryan pick it up and hold it."

"My, oh, my." Jared glanced at Courtney and winked before the door closed behind him. She watched them go down the steps and across the yard. Suddenly she turned off the fire, wiped her hands on a towel, and slipped on her jacket. When she reached them, they were standing inside the huge wire cage that was large enough to enclose two maple trees.

As she entered, Jared asked, "Who built this cage?"

"The park department," she said. "We have two of them. They're big and give the birds some freedom."

Ebeneezer was perched on a tree limb and eyed them silently while Guy whistled. "He did come when I whistled," Guy said.

Ryan glanced at Jared. "I think he's scared."

Jared readjusted the crutch under his arm and glared at the hawk. "I suppose the damned bird won't come down while I'm here."

"Let's step outside the cage," Courtney suggested.

They left and retreated to the tangle of brush that flanked the trail to the cage.

Guy whistled, and Ebeneezer tilted his head to one side, then with a lift of wings swooped down to perch on Guy's shoulder. Guy turned to smile at his dad.

"I'll be damned!" Jared whispered to Courtney. "Even so, he better leave my horses alone. They're worth too much for a rascally hawk to frighten them."

Ebeneezer squawked and ruffled his feathers.

"There's your answer," Courtney said dryly, and tried to smother a laugh.

"Same to you, bird," Jared said.

"Look at him, Dad. He'll let me pet him."

"Yeah, I see." Jared whispered to Courtney, "I think this was a damned conspiracy between you, your son, and that bird."

"I believe I can stop worrying quite so much about Ebeneezer from now on."

"Don't count on it."

She raised her voice. "Boys, how about hot chocolate?"

The fascination with Ebeneezer faded quickly with the offer of food, and both parents and sons returned to the house.

During the next hour, as they sat around the kitchen table, drinking hot chocolate and listening to Jared spin yarns about fishing trips, Courtney watched Ryan's eager face with a pang. This was the way a family should be, she thought, then felt a small shock that she had found companionship with Jared and his son. Both boys were laughing at something Jared had said. He waved his mug slightly and continued talking, his gaze meeting hers momentarily, holding her attention while he winked, giving her a silent message that he felt the same satisfaction she did.

His attention shifted to the boys, and she studied him openly. He had tipped back her kitchen chair, balancing himself on his good leg. Curly black chest hairs showed at the open neck of his gray shirt, and she imagined how soft they would feel to touch. Her gaze drifted upward over his firm jaw, his sensual mouth—to his smoldering blue eyes. Blushing, she looked down at her empty mug, turning it over in her hands while she heard a subtle change in his voice as he talked about a dog he once had. Within minutes the boys were laughing and she had relaxed, caught up in the story he was telling. And there wasn't the slightest trace of gruffness to him.

Finally, Jared stood up and said they had to get home to feed the horses and get dinner, but as they headed toward the door plans were made for the boys to get together after school again.

The boys spilled off the porch, racing to the truck, Guy's long legs giving him a lead. Jared's arm slipped around Courtney's waist, and he squeezed her lightly. She felt the bulge of muscles in his arm, caught a faint whiff of an enticing scent.

"Thanks for everything, kid," he said. "I know he brought it on himself, but you helped Guy over a rough spot."

"And Ryan is dazzled with your storytelling." She almost admitted she had been too.

He stopped to face her, his arm still casually around her waist. "See, I told you we fit together, kid. You and Ryan fill gaps we have—Guy and I do the same for you and Ryan."

Her breath stopped as her throat tightened. She couldn't agree because his blue eyes were sending an additional message. She wanted to get closer, to feel his arm tighten, to raise her lips to his.

"Dad, can Ryan come home with us for a while?" Guy called.

Jared smiled. "They have short memories," he said to Courtney.

She laughed. "It's a good thing." Raising her voice, she answered, "Sorry, Ryan. You need to stay home and do your homework."

Jared limped to the truck, and Ryan came to stand beside her, and together they watched the red pickup disappear down the road.

Seven

Friday morning Courtney received a call from the president of the county school P.T.A.

"Courtney, this is Myra Yates. The school carnival, our annual fund-raiser, is in March, remember?" Without waiting, Myra went on. "You've always been so good about helping. This year we need a chairman. I already have lots of volunteers, but no one can take the chair. I also need someone to volunteer to have the first meeting."

Courtney glanced at the books spread out on her kitchen table. "I don't mind having the meeting or being on a committee," she said, "but I'd prefer to take some task besides chairman."

"That's all right. When would a good meeting time be? I'll get the phone committee right on it."

"Next Tuesday morning, ten o'clock?"

"Excellent! I'll get back with you."

Myra Yates didn't call back until the next day. She told Courtney the meeting time was fine and asked if Courtney was willing to co-chair the committee. Courtney agreed, and when she hung up, she thought of Jared Calhoun. He had a son in school, but the P.T.A. was the last place on earth she expected to see Mr. Jared Calhoun.

So, when she opened her door a little before ten on Tuesday and found him on her porch, her heart jumped. She stared at him in shocked silence for a long moment. He was leaning against the door-jamb, filling the doorway with his broad shoulders, his crutch under his arm, and grinning from ear to ear. Beneath his sheepskin coat, he was wearing a pale blue western shirt that fit his broad chest and narrow waist perfectly. He had on jeans, mocca-sins, and his battered, broad-brimmed black hat sat squarely on his head.

"You don't belong to the P.T.A.!" Courtney said.

His grin widened. "What happened to 'hello' or 'good morning'?"

"Are you on this committee?"

"Put her there, kid." He extended a hand, which she ignored. He chuckled and placed his hand lightly on her shoulder. It seared as if it were a hot poker. Ignoring the sensations, wrestling with confusion and delight at seeing him again, she narrowed her eyes. "Have you ever been in the P.T.A. before?"

"Can't say that I have," he answered innocently.

"I knew it! You just did this to—" She broke off abruptly, and he leaned closer.

"To what, kid?"

"To tease me!"

He chuckled. "No, that wasn't my motive." His eyes developed a devilish twinkle and, dropping his voice to a suggestive tone, he asked, "Want to know why I'm here?"

"Never mind! You're early too!"

"I couldn't wait."

"Oh, balderdash. Come in."

"Such southern hospitality. Freeze the—"

"Never mind!"

He grinned again and entered the house, the crisp, cool air coming with him, and she felt as if her home was being taken over.

"May I take your coat and hat?" she said.

"Sure thing." He smiled pleasantly as he pulled off the sheepskin jacket and placed his hat on top of it. He handed them to her, and their fingers brushed in this routine she had followed with guests for years. Only this time it wasn't routine. She was conscious of Jared's slightest touch and felt her mouth go dry at the sight of his soft navy sweater hugging his broad chest. She put down his things hastily.

As he followed her down the wide front hall to the high-ceilinged living room, Jared looked around with open curiosity. In the living room Courtney glanced at the familiar surroundings she had barely given a thought to, other than cleaning, in so long.

For the first time she noticed how feminine the living room was. The big windows had white eyelet tier curtains. The floor was covered by a rose-colored carpet, the sofa was a soft rose velvet, and there were two beige wing chairs by an upright piano. With the exception of an overstuffed brown chair and hassock, the room was almost dainty in appearance. It was spotlessly neat and clean with a Dresden figurine on the mantle, a crystal vase on a table, and a few potted plants. Jared's gaze settled on her.

"Is your son's room pink too?" he asked.

"No, it isn't!" she snapped. "You can go see it, if you're so darned curious!"

"All right, lead the way."

Instantly she knew she had walked into a trap.

She didn't want to show him Ryan's room, take him through the house, past her bedroom.

"You don't really want to see . . ."

"It is pink," he said softly, and shook his head.

"It's not! I'll show you."

She left the room, and he followed her. Her back tingled, every nerve coming alive as she imagined his gaze on her. She wanted to smooth her fuzzy white sweater, to touch her hair, but she resisted the impulse and slowed to walk beside him down the hall.

"This is a nice house," he said. "You grew up here?"

"Yes. My father was a professor at Vanderbilt University, and shortly after I was born, my grandmother's health became poor. We moved back here to live so Mom could help take care of her. My great-aunt never married and later she came to live with us too. Dad died when I was eleven. You grew up in a household of men, I grew up in a household of women. My first encounter with the outside world was college."

"Which college?"

"Vanderbilt."

"Years after I went."

She laughed. "How many years?"

"I'm thirty-seven. I was at Vanderbilt a long time ago."

"You must have set some professors on their ears."

He chuckled and touched her cheek. "I'm not that difficult."

"Of course not. I majored in English, but I didn't finish. I got married instead. What did you major in?"

"I have a degree in electrical engineering," he said casually, and it surprised her. "What was your father's field?" he added.

"English. He was Dr. Raines, and he taught Tennyson, Browning, Shakespeare, medieval literature, that sort of thing. Did you work as an engineer?"

"Yep, but I quit to go into the real estate business with Leah. We met at Vanderbilt. She was from Memphis. We were married twelve years."

"It's difficult to imagine you selling real estate."

"Commercial is different from residential." His eyes sparkled. "I have my moments of congeniality."

They reached the open door to her room and she stared straight ahead, trying to think of something to say. "Ebeneezer is locked up securely," was all she could come up with.

Jared paused and turned into her room, asking with all innocence, "Is this Ryan's room?"

"No, it's not."

He stood in the bedroom, looking around while she remained in the hall. Why had she let him talk her into a tour of the house?

"This is your room," he said huskily. "It's like you."

She wasn't about to ask how.

"Scared to come in here with me?"

"No. I'm waiting. I thought you wanted to see Ryan's room."

He grinned. "Not really. I wanted to see yours," he admitted.

"You're so darned irritating! Let's go back to the living room." How could she get him out of her room?

"Kid, I bet you wear white cotton granny gowns to bed." His grin widened.

"That's definitely none of your business!" She hated the blush that crept up her cheeks.

"But I'm right. Your pink cheeks give you away. Want to know what I wear?"

"No!"

He chuckled. "Still leading with your chin." He crossed to the bed and sat down—and was lost to her sight. She stepped to the door. The sight of him seated on her bed made her pulse pound. He was so blatantly masculine; his presence invaded her senses.

"Will you get off my bed?"

"Don't get so huffy. I'm not touching you or threatening you. I'm just sitting on your bed. Bad for the springs, but it doesn't hurt you. I want to see where you sleep."

"I'll be in the living room."

"Wait a minute," he said, amused. "I'm just satisfying my curiosity. I didn't mean to frighten you."

"I'm not frightened." She crossed the room and faced him squarely with her hands on her hips. "I don't know why you persist! We're as different as night and day. You don't like the way I live, and goodness knows, I don't like the way you live!"

He stood up. "You're not all that intimidated when it gets right down to basics. And we have moments when we get along just dandy. We had a good time the other day with the boys."

"Yes, we did."

"I wondered if you'd admit it." His eyes twinkled. "I can't resist teasing; I know I'll get a rise out of you." He reached out and placed his hand lightly on her throat. Her pulse jumped with his touch, and his brow arched. "That's another reason, kid. There's a chemistry between us that you're as aware of as I am. It's marvelous. And beneath your cool, skittish exterior is a passionate woman. I hate waste."

"We should go back to the living room."

"See, your pulse is ready for takeoff, motors revved."

"No, it's not," she denied, but it came out weakly,

and she knew he was right. He was standing too close, and she felt drawn to him, as if invisible cords were pulling her closer. The doorbell rang. "Now you have to come," she said. "I'm not answering the door with you in my bedroom."

He laughed. "Course not! Wouldn't want to sully your spotless reputation. And I'll bet it's spotless! Who're you dating?"

"I don't. The doorbell's ringing."

"Shall we answer it?"

She turned away, mildly irritated with herself. She wished she could relax around Jared, handle his teasing casually, but it wasn't her nature. She waited in the hall for him to join her, then they walked to the front door. Four women were waiting on the porch. Within fifteen minutes the other ladies had arrived, introductions had been made, and everyone was seated in the living room while Courtney served coffee and sweet rolls. Jared was sitting in the overstuffed chair, his injured foot on the hassock, the center of attention.

Myra Yates, shaking back her long red hair, gushed sweetly, "It's so wonderful to have a man's support on this project, Jared. You didn't say anything on the phone about your foot. How did you hurt it?"

"When Courtney attacked me," he said, "I accidentally shot myself."

Courtney spilled the cream as she almost dropped the tray she was carrying in from the kitchen. "That isn't so!" she exclaimed.

Everyone stared at her. Myra laughed nervously and wriggled in her chair. "Well, I can't wait to hear what happened."

"I was minding my own business," Jared obligingly explained, "standing on my property when Courtney came flying across the fence at me—"

"—When you tried to kill my son's pet. And my

foot hit the fence and threw me off-balance!"
Courtney interrupted.

Brows were raised all around the room, but if it
bothered Jared Calhoun, he didn't reveal it. He
just smiled. "A hawk that attacked my horses.
Some pet. Damned vicious bird." He gave the
ladies the benefit of his full smile and received a
half-dozen smiles in return.

Disgusted, Courtney went back to the kitchen to
clean up the mess on the tray and get more cream.
When she entered the living room again, Jared had
everyone laughing. As she served she listened to
the women ply him with questions and laugh at
his answers. She sat down on one of the wooden
kitchen chairs, as far away from Jared Calhoun as
possible and sipped black coffee, waiting for Myra
Yates to start the meeting. No one seemed to be in a
hurry, though; they all appeared to prefer listening
to Jared.

Courtney stared out the window, but her full
attention was in the room. Maybe it was just the
novelty of having a man at a P.T.A. meeting, she
thought. The women were dithering and fussing
over Jared, and he was as charming as a sunny
day. Where were the fiery sparks that were generated when it was just the two of them?

"Would you care for more coffee, Jared?"
Annabel Whitley asked, and rose to carry the tray
to him, ignoring five women on the way.

He smiled and helped himself.

"Oh, do have a roll. They're so delicious,
Courtney!" Tina Smith said without once taking
her eyes from Jared.

Declining the roll, he took charge, turning to
Myra and asking, "Shall we call the meeting to
order now, Myra?"

"Of course." She straightened a notebook on her

lap and flashed a big smile at Jared as she called the meeting to order.

The minutes were read, the treasurer's report was given, and old business was settled. Then Myra asked for new business and began to outline plans for the annual school carnival with the cochairmen, Jared and Courtney. Everyone soon began talking at once, making suggestions, and Courtney heard Annabel ask Jared, "Is your foot comfortable?"

"It's fine," he said.

"Have some more coffee, Jared," Tina said, refilling his cup.

Courtney closed her eyes in disgust. It was probably one of the few times during the year that any liquid except beer had crossed his lips.

She opened her eyes to find Jared watching her while he listened to Myra talk about refreshments. He looked amused until the moment their gazes locked. An invisible current seemed to leap across the room and electrify the air, shutting out the rest of the world.

Voices became a dim undercurrent of noise. The temperature in the room increased until it was difficult for Courtney to breathe; she was held fast by clear blue eyes. His attention lowered to her mouth. Her lips parted, the tip of her tongue touched the corner of her mouth, then, realizing what she was doing, she closed her mouth quickly.

Jared raised an eyebrow and smiled, making her blush.

Her thoughts were interrupted as she heard someone say, "Don't you think so, Courtney?"

"Hmmm? Oh, yes."

"Good. We'll put you down to take care of the decorations."

"I'll help her," Jared said, grinning.

Courtney straightened. What was the matter with her?

"Jared and Courtney are in charge of the decorations," Myra said. "Now, who'll volunteer to supervise the three-legged race?"

"Think I'm out of that one," Jared said, and there were several giggles.

Courtney began to wonder if the morning would ever end. And when it did, she knew Jared Calhoun would not be the first to leave. Finally the meeting drew to a close, and as everyone began to stand she turned to Myra.

"Myra, you'll pass Jared's place on your way home. He raises Tennessee Walking Horses. You should stop and let him show them to you."

Before anyone could answer, Jared cut in smoothly. "Come out Sunday at three. I have some other people coming then. Today they're out to pasture and you won't see anything except an empty barn. Besides, I want to stay and help my cochairman do the dishes."

Courtney's heart jumped. She was flustered enough and didn't want him to stay and tease her more. "That's not necessary!" she snapped.

"I have the next meeting," Tina said quickly. "You can help with my dishes."

Jared laughed and Courtney smiled frostily, fighting the urge to tell Tina to take him home with her right now.

While he stood on the porch and said good-bye to the women as if he were the host and it were his house, Courtney picked up his jacket and hat. She returned to the porch, set them down behind him, then waved and closed and locked the door, all without a word to Mr. Jared Calhoun.

She waited, expecting him to pound on the door. Nothing happened. Maybe he could take a hint, she thought, although she was surprised that he acquiesced so readily to something that didn't fit his plans. She went into the living room and peeked out the window. A cloud of dust was hanging in the air on the road, but all the cars were out of sight, including Jared's red truck.

Relief filled Courtney. She had been on pins throughout the entire meeting, and it irritated her that he continued to have such a disturbing effect. She gathered up the dishes, stacking them on the tray, and carried them out to the kitchen. When she entered that room, the first thing she saw was Jared, sitting at the table, one foot propped on a chair, smiling at her.

Eight

She almost dropped the tray a second time. "How did you get in here?"

"Such a warm reception. I came in the back door. I'm not ready to go home. I'll help with the dishes."

"Thanks, but you can't walk and there's not much to do." He stood up, and she held the tray in front of her as if it were a shield. "Did you ever hear of overstaying your welcome?"

"Yep, kid, but I won't do that."

"Ha! Don't come any closer."

"Why, oh, why, do you act like a young and very nervous virgin around me?"

She plunked the tray onto the table, rattling dishes and spilling cream again. "I act like a normal woman who's in the company of an obstreperous codger!"

He advanced, and she wanted to run. While she forced herself to stand still, his words ran through her mind like salt over a wound. Nervous virgin! Damn him!

Her pulse was at a full gallop now, and her mouth became dry at the heat in Jared's eyes. "You send my blood pressure to a dangerous level," she said.

"There we have something in common. You send mine to a dangerous level, too, kid. You call me crusty—I think you're the crusty one! And it's only on the surface." His voice lowered. "All morning you've felt the same thing I have."

She didn't have to ask what. She knew, and she was torn by two entirely different feelings. She wanted to tell him to go, yet at the same time she wanted to walk into his arms and raise her lips for his kiss.

"You haven't listened to anything I've said," she said.

"You're too passionate to act like an icicle."

"Icicle! Dammit, how's this, Jared Calhoun?" She reached for him, seeing the flare of surprise—or was it satisfaction?—in his expression. She locked her arms around his neck, pressed her lips firmly on his, and kissed him for all she was worth. And he returned the kiss, perhaps for all he was worth. It seemed that way to Courtney, because she felt jolted, as if by an explosion. She burned and trembled and responded as his tongue thrust deeply, then stroked so leisurely, becoming a pleasure that erased his accusation. It was an effort to remember that she was trying to prove a point. Finally she pulled away, and her voice came out a breathless whisper.

"Now, will you go home?"

"Not in a million years," he said huskily. "That was the kind of kiss a man dreams about."

"Was it the kiss of an icicle?"

"I'm not sure. Let's try again, and I'll give you an

answer." As a smile reached her lips, his head dipped down for another kiss and his arms tightened, crushing her to him. He leaned over her, molding her soft curves to his hard leanness. The fit was perfect, taking her breath, making her moan as she kissed him wildly.

Without a pause in the kiss, he sat down and pulled her onto his lap. His hand stroked her back, moving slowly along her spine, his fingers lightly feeling each vertebra, pressing sensuously against the curve in the small of her back, sliding around her narrow waist, and rising to brush the full, up-thrusting curve of her breast.

Courtney whimpered softly. A dizzying feeling was racing through her, and she clung to his shoulders. She had to stop him! He was something she couldn't handle, yet there were moments when it seemed so right to be with him.

His fingers brushed lightly across the throbbing peak of her breast, and it was as if he had turned on an electrical current in her veins. She gasped and shifted, pushing away.

"You have to go!"

She stood up and straightened her clothes, then looked down at him. His smoldering gaze almost buckled her knees, and she tried to remain stern, to remember the peppers and his rascally disposition, and forget his teasing banter, his sexiness, and his riveting blue eyes.

"You really want me to leave?" he asked.

"You make me nervous! You may kiss like a dream, but you're a cigar-smoking, beer-drinking, pepper-guzzling man!" She gasped for breath.

"I may cry," he said with a grin.

"Ha! Your sensitivity probably burned up in the pepper sauce."

"When was the last time you saw me smoke a cigar?"

"I don't remember. Last week?"

"I gave them up."

"You did?" She was shocked. She wanted to ask, yet hated to. Curiosity won. "Why?"

His blue eyes twinkled. "Bad for my health."

"That they are."

"And someone I respect doesn't like them."

She caught her breath. Had he given up cigars for her?

"You won't ask, will you?" He laughed softly. "I gave them up because you don't like them."

"My goodness!"

"That doesn't quite describe it. But I figure it's worth the sacrifice." He stood up. "Bye, kid. Come see me when you get lonesome."

"Sure enough."

Laughing, he touched her chin—and she almost tipped her head to brush his knuckles with her lips!

"When hell freezes over, huh?" he said.

"Could be," she murmured, thinking about the cigars. Jared Calhoun had given up his cigars because she didn't like them? He figured it was worth the sacrifice?

Suddenly he leaned down to peer intently into her eyes. "What does it take to make you laugh, Courtney Meade?"

"Something nice and laughable," she answered, but his question startled her, and she realized how seldom she laughed nowadays.

"I'll work on it. Bye, kid." And he was gone, leaving a strange emptiness behind him. The house had changed. His presence lingered. She went to her room and looked at the bed. The spread was still rumpled where he had sat down. What was it about Jared Calhoun that reached beneath the surface and held the strings of her heart? she wondered. He had given up his cigars for her! No man had made a sacrifice like that for her. The implications made her pulse drum. He wasn't always crusty, that she had to admit.

The next afternoon as she pulled cherry pie from the oven Courtney glanced out the window for the dozenth time, aware that it was thirty minutes before Ryan would appear. She drew her breath in sharply when she saw the red pickup come up the drive and stop. Jared Calhoun's long denim-clad legs, his crutch, and his boots appeared as he climbed out, and Admiral jumped down from the back of the truck.

As she went outside she tried to ignore the fluttering that changed her heartbeat. "What are you doing here?" she asked when he reached the porch.

"Such a welcome." A big, innocent smile appeared. "I came to study the birds."

"You didn't!"

"I can't look?"

"Yes, but you're here for another reason."

"Why do you think I'm here?"

"To see the birds!" She blushed and then laughed. "Maybe to see someone."

"Ahh, progress! I came to look at the sanctuary, to see you, to talk to you, to be with you. How's that?"

"Nice," she answered with honesty.

"Will you show me around?"

"Let me get a jacket." She stepped inside and snatched up her tan jacket, pausing to look at herself in the mirror. She smoothed the short tendrils of hair that had escaped from her long braid, then went back out to lead Jared along one of the trails. The many trees, along with the sumac and tall brown grasses, provided a dense tangle that lined the winding dirt path. The quiet was broken only by the soft sound of their footsteps and bird calls.

When they reached a wide place in the trail, Jared paused to look at the bird-observation area. A tall wooden barrier had small peepholes cut at various heights to accommodate both children and adults. When Jared bent over to look through an opening, she noticed the long length of his legs, the soft denim molding to his muscles. He straightened.

"Sign in there says, 'U.S. Department of the Interior banding station,' " he said. "Are you a bander?"

"Yes," she answered as they continued on the trail. It narrowed, and Jared moved closer, his shoulder touching hers as they walked. "I finished my year's apprenticeship a long time ago," she continued. "As a matter of fact, I did some banding this morning."

"You put a mist net up in that area?"

Surprised, she halted. "You've banded birds?"

"I'd like to say yes, but I haven't. Leah was a bander when she belonged to the Audubon Society, and I went with her occasionally." They crossed a wooden bridge over a narrow creek of rushing water. When the trail broadened to accommodate an iron bench near a bird feeder, Jared caught her hand.

"Let's sit a spell," he said softly, and settled on the bench, placing his crutch carefully beside him.

She sat down, aware of his arms stretched behind her across the back of the bench, his thigh so close to her own. On the opposite side of the trail was a tall bare-limbed hackberry with a birdhouse nailed to the rough gray trunk. After a moment of quiet, birds began to flit among the bare branches nearby.

"Did the park department furnish the bird-houses?" Jared asked.

"No. We operate on a shoestring. I built them with my handy saw."

"Son-of-a-gun! I'll know where to come for help when I build a shed next summer."

"Well, don't look too closely at the construction."

They sat quietly for a few minutes until Jared said, "It's peaceful out here."

"I know. Sometimes I come sit here during the day. It's cool and nice in the summertime. Right now it's a little chilly."

"Cold?" He dropped his arm around her and pulled her close.

"No, I'm comfortable," she answered with a smile, relishing his touch.

"Shucks, I hoped you'd say you're freezing."

She laughed softly, and his smile broadened. "That's better," he said. "I know how a photographer feels trying to elicit some kind of a smile from a baby."

"Oh, my goodness, you think I'm that stern? And of all people—you're so gruff."

"Who? Me?"

She laughed again, and his arm tightened a fraction. "Better."

"You'll scare the birds away."

"I'd rather hear your laughter." He raised his voice. "Pipe down, birds, let me hear the kid laugh!"

And she did while birds fluttered out of the nearest tree. "See what you did!"

His voice lowered. "Look, the next two weekends we have meetings to work on the school carnival, then the carnival is the following Saturday. I know it'll be the middle of March, but the first free Saturday night, let's go somewhere nice for dinner. For a few hours, you forget what's in my refrigerator; I'll forget you attacked me and made me shoot myself."

As she took a deep breath she gazed into eyes as blue as a summer sky. He smiled and his voice was coaxing when he said, "Dinner in Nashville, somewhere quiet and elegant."

She understood now why women fussed over him. "What time?"

"Eight o'clock."

"All right, if I can get a sitter for Ryan," she said breathlessly. "It's difficult to get someone to come out here. I have a friend from church, Mrs. Bartlett, who comes sometimes and sleeps over. She's almost an adopted grandmother to Ryan. I'll see if she can come."

"Good. Guy can stay with his cousins at Lonnie's." He grinned. "And for one evening we'll forget all the things we know about each other . . . and we'll learn a whole new set of things."

"I'll try," she said with an unexpected surge of excitement.

He stood up, adjusted his crutch, and reached his hand out to her. "Shall we go back?"

"Yes. The school bus will be along shortly."

"I hope you don't mind. I told Guy I'd be here so he'll be getting off with Ryan."

"You did? Well, I hope they don't fight."

"They won't."

As Courtney and Jared circled back to the house Ryan and Guy came up the drive. Both boys waved while Admiral bounded down to meet them, and once again Courtney thought briefly how like a family they appeared.

Jared's soft voice startled her. "Kind of nice like this, isn't it?"

"Yes, it is," she answered. "I'm glad they get along."

"Give two boys a football or turtle to look at and they usually forget their differences."

"Maybe that's what we need. Something simple to forget ours," she said dryly.

"Kid, I don't ever want to forget the differences between you and me. They're the most fascinating differences in the world." His eyes were intense, altering her breathing until Guy interrupted, calling to them.

"Hey, Dad, look what we found. A fossil!"

They all studied a rock that bore a slight resemblance to a fossil, then Courtney offered to fix a snack and all four started toward the house.

"Boys," Jared said, "let's go look at old Ebeneezer until the snacks are ready."

"Yes, sir," Ryan said solemnly, handing his books to Courtney. Guy plunked his on the porch, and the two boys walked beside Jared toward the cages. Courtney noticed how Jared's brown hair glinted in the light, how the wind stirred locks of it as he disappeared around the trail with the boys. She hummed as she washed her hands, and a thread of anticipation tickled her as she continually glanced out the window to watch for their return.

Half an hour later they sat down in the kitchen to drink milk and eat warm cherry pie. "Mom," Ryan said, "Mr. Calhoun said he would let me ride one of his horses. He said he'd take me to see them now if you'll let me go."

"You don't know how to ride a horse." She glanced at Jared, whose wide blue eyes were as guileless as a daisy.

"He'll learn," Jared replied.

"Ryan, don't you have homework?"

"I can get it done tonight. Let me, Mom."

"Sure she will, Ryan," Jared said. "My horses are

a sight to see. I'll take care of him," he added to Courtney.

"Did you ever break your leg?" Guy asked.

"Let's discuss your broken leg later, Guy," Jared said smoothly, but Courtney wasn't going to be put off.

"I'd like to hear about it. How'd you break your leg, Guy?"

"Fell off a horse."

"He was much younger, and Ryan won't fall off. We'll be very careful."

"Please, Mom."

Three males waited, watching her hopefully. "I suppose," she said, and received three grins.

"Wait until you ride Zorro," Guy said.

"Is he scary?"

"Naw, he hardly moves." While the boys discussed the merits of the horses, Jared winked at Courtney. She refilled glasses with milk and served more pie that disappeared rapidly. Finally they got up from the table, told her good-bye, and left.

When the red pickup returned two hours later, Jared let Ryan out, waved, and drove away. Through dinner, Courtney listened to Ryan talk about horses, about learning to ride, about Zorro and Apollo. She learned that Ryan hoped to go to Jared's the following day to ride—and realized the ties between them were growing stronger.

Throughout the next week Ryan rode at Jared's every afternoon. In the evening both families ate together, either at Jared's or Courtney's, and the bond of closeness grew along with her awareness of Jared Calhoun as an appealing man. She noticed his strong brown hands as he held an injured bird, his long arms when he reached high into the kitchen cabinets to get something for her, his sensuous, well-shaped lips that made her mouth go dry when she thought about his kisses.

On the first weekend in March they worked at Jefferson Davis school, painting and constructing booths for the carnival. The following Tuesday morning a cold north wind was blowing gray clouds across the sky and light flakes of snow were falling when Courtney braided her hair and changed from her white flannel nightgown into faded jeans and a red sweater. She pulled on her brown parka and went outside to feed Ebeneezer. Chill from the weather changed to icy fear when she found the cage open and the hawk gone. Gritting her teeth she ran to her Jeep.

As she sped up Jared's drive her heart lurched. Light snow was swirling over a row of vehicles parked in the drive; Jared's black Ford sedan and his pickup, a red sports car, and a yellow sedan. Two men in topcoats and suits were standing outside the corral beside Jared Calhoun. She stopped breathing when she saw Jared. He was wearing his sheepskin coat and jeans, and his black hat was pulled down over his eyes. His crutch was leaning against his side, and he was holding a flapping hawk. As Courtney drove nearer the men turned to watch her while Jared tried to get a better grip on the hawk.

Thoughts, choices of action, flashed through Courtney's mind. Ebeneezer was about to have his neck wrung! There wasn't time to reason, so she did the only thing she could think to do. She leaned on the horn and aimed the Jeep for a spot about two feet behind Jared Calhoun. At the sound of the horn he looked up, his eyes widening as she headed toward him.

Nine

The two men ran. At the last moment, Jared jumped out of the way, lost his balance, and fell, loosening his hold on the hawk. Ebeneezer flew skyward, swiftly putting distance between himself and Jared.

Courtney slammed on the brakes. She took a deep breath of cold air that was changing from indigo blue to deep purple with oaths.

"Calhoun, you tried to kill Ebeneezer!" she shouted as she stepped down from the Jeep.

"Dammit to hell, kid, you tried to kill *me*!"

"Want me to call the sheriff, Mr. Calhoun?" one man asked, starting toward the house, his breath vaporizing with his question.

"No." Jared stood with amazing ease. He picked up his crutch. "You tried to run me down with a Jeep!"

"No, I didn't! I tried to attract your attention. I was several feet away!"

He swore in a flat, angry voice while he moved closer. Her heartbeat jumped at his proximity and fiery blue eyes.

"You said you'd keep that damned bird in a cage!" he said.

"He got loose somehow. Ryan must have left the latch unfastened."

"He's scared two of my horses away. I'm on crutches, thanks to you. I don't feel like riding through the brush, hunting two horses!"

"I'll do it for you, but you leave my hawk alone! Don't you wring his neck!"

"Mr. Calhoun," one of the men said, "perhaps we should come back another time to look at the horses."

"I'll be with y'all in just a moment. I need to settle something with Mrs. Meade. By the way, this is Mr. Waring and Mr. Sampson. This is Mrs. Meade, my hotheaded neighbor, the one who caused my injury."

Mr. Waring paled and moved toward his car. "We'll come back, Mr. Calhoun."

"Don't go. Mrs. Meade isn't annoyed with either of you."

"Now see here!" Courtney said. "It wasn't like that, and you know it!" Her temper boiled over. "You're a pain in the neck! Tell them the truth! You shot yourself."

Turning to the two men, Jared shrugged. "I didn't press charges."

"Oh! If that isn't the limit! Tell them the truth!"

Jared waved his hand at the two men, who were openly staring at Courtney. "I won't be long," he said. "Go up to the house and have a seat. We'll have a beer in a minute." His blue eyes nailed her. "As soon as I'm finished here."

"We'll come back when it isn't snowing," Mr.

Sampson said. "We'll call. Er, nice to have met you, Mrs. Meade."

"You don't need to go because of me. I won't be here long," she said.

"I'll call you Monday, all right?" Jared asked them.

"Sure, Jared." With curious glances at Courtney, the men climbed into their cars and drove away.

"If you don't want ole Ebeneezer Hawk boiled, keep him home!" Jared said. He leaned closer, his eyes snapping and his jaw thrust forward.

"I don't know how he got out, but the door to his cage was open."

"I don't *care* how he gets out. Next time, you might be home instead of trying to run me down."

"I didn't try to run you down."

"Like hell. It was close to attempted man-slaughter."

"Oh, for goodness sake!"

"Wow, kid, you gotta watch your language there." She couldn't be sure, but she thought the devilish twinkle had returned to his eyes.

"I'll try to find your horses."

"No thanks! Don't you go near my horses! You're lucky I'm injured, otherwise you might have found yourself in hot water."

"How's that? Same tactics as your son? Are you going to slug me? I wouldn't put it past you!" The twinkle was definitely there.

"You need to learn a lesson, kid. You came within a foot of running over me."

"I was farther away than that! I would think you'd feel terrible if you killed a little boy's pet."

"The world's full of hawks, and that one is mean as Lucifer."

"How would you feel if I tried to wring Admiral's neck?"

"That isn't the same. A bird and a dog are two

different critters. Besides, I was going to put him in a box and let Guy bring him back home."

"Hah! And the daisies are blooming today all over Tennessee!"

He grinned. "I thought it was a magnanimous action on my part. I didn't know I'd almost lose my life for it." He moved closer, and she stepped back.

"Now, Mr. Calhoun . . ."

"You should've thought of that possibility before you came charging at me like a bat out of hell." He stepped closer while she moved back until she bumped into the Jeep.

"I didn't drive right for you, and I had to rescue Ebeneezer. I'm going home. I'll put Ebeneezer in his cage as soon—" A long arm stretched out and blocked her.

"You ran me down, I fell. If I'd had a gun, I could've shot someone or one of my horses. My foot hurts like hell now, and you say, 'Ta, ta, I'm going home'? Bull." He was so close now she could feel the warmth of his body.

"Get back!" she said.

His eyes sparkled, although his mouth firmed. He shifted his weight, moving his crutch slightly. "I really wasn't going to wring the hawk's neck."

"Please, spare me the nonsense! Will you move your arm?"

"Sure." Crinkles fanned from the corners of his eyes, and his arm went around her waist.

"Oh, dear, you do have a way . . ." It was difficult to talk. His mouth was inches away, his eyes were smoldering, and his arm was tight.

"Kid, I'm gonna get retribution, the sweetest kind." He leaned forward, across the last bit of space, and his lips brushed hers, igniting a fire that heated her limbs. He drew her to him, pressing her softness against him.

She placed her hands on his broad chest and

pushed. His arm merely tightened, and his mouth came down fully.

Courtney struggled—for about one-tenth of a second—then Jared's tongue invaded her mouth, and she was lost. Dimly, she wondered why she had such a violent, instant reaction to a man like Jared Calhoun, but then the question swirled away like snowflakes in the wind. A storm was buffeting her, a storm of sensation that was delicious, hot, and sent logic to oblivion.

Suddenly he stopped, so swiftly that she blinked. She felt dazed.

"Kid, it was worth almost getting run over." He smiled for the first time, a smug male smile that made her cheeks burn.

"For someone so damned sexy—" She bit her lip.

His grin widened. "Yeah? Do go on. I can't wait to hear the rest!"

"Get out of my way."

"So damned sexy . . . Ummm, that does give me hope."

"Well, don't let it! It was a slip. I'm just dumbfounded that anyone who can be so cussed difficult can kiss the way you do!"

His grin widened. "Kid, you're cute when you're angry."

"You're not!"

"I'm not angry." He sounded as if he were fighting laughter.

"You're not cute either."

"Mercy, that's a relief!"

"Get out of my way!" Her anger was beginning to fizzle. She felt a smile about to surface and knew it would stir Jared Calhoun's arrogant satisfaction.

"Want another kiss before you go?"

"No, dammit!"

"Ahh. You'll get over your inhibitions if you stick around long enough, kid."

She closed her eyes for a moment. "Of all people to buy the property next door . . ."

"You can move. It's a free world."

"You know my family has lived on that property for over a century! Why am I doing this? Get out of my way."

He hunched his shoulders, lost his smile, and looked her straight in the eye. "Wait a second, kid . . ."

Her heart lurched at the tone of his voice. Then it skipped beats as he pulled her against him and kissed her soundly again. And had the same devastating effect. She forgot herself, winding her arms around his neck as if he were an ordinary man.

He definitely wasn't ordinary in any way. And neither were his kisses. She wanted to melt into his arms, to press against his lean hardness, to return his kiss, to hold him tightly.

When he finally stopped, she looked up at him and tried to get her breath and her wits. "You defy all laws of nature," she said. "You should smell like beer, kiss like an ape, and be as appealing as Attila the Hun."

"Instead?" he asked with a twinkle in his eyes.

"Fishing, Mr. Calhoun?"

"I smell like . . ."

She felt as if she were on fire, and as if she were floating. She wanted to reach for him and barely heard what he had said. Her thoughts were tumbling in a whirling jumble as she tried to sort out why he was so marvelous to kiss, why the verbal sparring was pure excitement. She answered without thinking. ". . . like clover, like something nice . . ."

His voice was soft, a coaxing whisper. "And my kiss?"

That jolted her to awareness. "Was an intrusion! Will you get out of my way?"

"I'm scared to death, kid." He grinned. "I'll move, but you tell me about my kiss."

"Like hell, to use your phrase."

"I'll just have to imagine what you think."

"Don't."

"I smell nice. Encouraging."

"Forget it! Are we going to stand here all day?"

"Scared?"

"Irritated!"

"Yeah, I know how irritated you were a minute ago."

She blushed hotly and climbed behind the Jeep's steering wheel. He reached out to take her chin and turn her face to his.

"Guess it's been worth almost getting run over. Kiss me good-bye, kid."

"I just did!" She started to jerk free, but his fingers tightened, then his lips touched hers, and he didn't have to hold her any longer.

Finally, he raised his head a little. "You know, if your kisses were as prudish and prim as your conversation, I would've washed my hands of you long ago, but your kisses sizzle." He looked at her intently, and his voice, which lowered with each word, was full of curiosity. "You're a complicated package, Courtney Meade. Your words are like snow, your kisses fire . . . You seem so complex."

His husky words trailed through her system like heated wine, diffusing into her bloodstream, making her giddy. His own personality had plenty of contradictions. And yet he could be so sensuous and tender.

She shook her head as if trying to clear away cobwebs.

"You know what I want?" he asked, his voice deep.

"What?"

"Someday I want to hold you and love you," he said solemnly.

Her breath failed for an instant as she gazed into his eyes. "Why don't you date some of the women who fuss so over you?" she whispered. "That nurse, Tina—I've seen them all but drool."

"I'm far more intrigued with my sweet neighbor."

Sweet? she repeated to herself. He sounded sincere. She blinked in astonishment and realized he really was enjoying himself. And she had to admit she was too. "I'm sweet! That isn't what you said a few minutes ago. I remember words about manslaughter—"

He shrugged. "We have our moments. But you care about people," he said softly. His fingers drifted along her throat lightly. "You cared about Guy even when he annoyed the hell out of you. You care about a damned hawk. You just care about the creatures around you. I've had all the indifference I can stand in my lifetime.

"*And* I don't feel the same thing around other women." His forefinger traced the line of her collar, making her draw a sharp breath. "There, see. You feel it too when we touch."

"That's physical. We're both in vulnerable situations."

A lazy smile crossed his features. "I'll have to admit, kid, your personality isn't bland. When you get right down to it, you're kind of fun. A little prim, but we're working on it."

She had started to thank him until he added the last. "Well," she said, "your pesky attitude toward Ebeneezer, I can't call fun."

His eyes sparkled, but he looked at her seriously. "My kisses are."

"Humph!" She bit back a smile. Mr. Jared

Calhoun was really getting to her. "Darned arrogant too!"

"And, according to my son, you bake the best cherry pie in Tennessee."

"Guy said that?" she asked, startled and pleased.

"Yep. I'll have to agree. And maybe he does need a better diet."

"Will wonders never cease?"

He grinned, and she remembered what she was doing. "I'm going home now!"

He stepped away while she turned the ignition. The engine made a grinding noise and died. And her spirits died right along with it. She glanced at him and saw him purse his lips.

"Dammit, it would be just my luck . . ." she whispered.

"Say something, kid?"

"No!" She tried again. The same grating noise sounded, then silence. Snow whirled down, sliding down the windshield, falling on Jared's hat brim and over his broad shoulders. She tried another time while her face turned red.

"Want me to try?" he asked with a smile.

"Drat it!"

"Watch your language, kid. Get out and I'll try."

She stepped out. He tried, with the same result, then climbed out and raised the hood. She watched as he leaned over, standing on his good foot, holding his other foot in the air while he tinkered with something beneath the hood.

"I've been having trouble starting it," she said. "I've had trouble with the Jeep and the plumbing and the furnace. If it isn't one thing, it's two or three."

He worked in silence, then tried several more times to start the Jeep. "I think you need a new flywheel in the starter," he said as he slid out of the Jeep.

"Dammit!"

He gazed skyward as if he saw something interesting besides hundreds of snowflakes, and she wondered if he were hiding laughter.

"Are you laughing at me?"

"Not one hee-haw has crossed my lips," he said solemnly as he took her arm. "I don't know about you, but I'm frozen. Come inside, we'll have some coffee."

"I can walk home if you don't mind my leaving the Jeep here."

"Hell's bells, kid. Come in the house and have some hot coffee."

She was chilled and miserable and hadn't dressed warmly enough to walk home.

"All right. My feet are freezing."

"Yeah. Mine too."

"Doesn't that make your injured foot hurt?"

"Sure as hell does." He looked at the sky again. "We're in for it."

"What about your horses?"

"They've been fed. They have enough sense to wander back to the barn."

"Then why did you get so mad at Ebeneezer?"

"He causes me trouble. Damned bird. I don't like to be interfered with by a bird. Feathery kind, that is."

"Are you calling me a bird?"

"What gave you that idea?" he asked with great innocence.

"I think maybe I'd rather walk home with sneakers and cold feet."

"Pish-tosh, to use one of your vintage expressions."

She laughed, and they went inside. The warmth of the kitchen felt good. Something smelled delicious, and she guessed he had a roast in the oven. They removed their coats, and her gaze lingered on his broad shoulders covered in a pale blue woolen shirt, and his faded, tight jeans. "I like red," he said, assessing her more thoroughly. He pulled out a chair and sat down, then swore.

"What's wrong? Does your foot hurt?"

"Yep. It's the cold."

"Let me get the coffee. I didn't know you had any."

"Bought it just for you."

She turned around, startled. "You didn't know I'd be here!" Her words faded at the piercing look in his eyes. The invisible current that was so volatile sparked between them and she knew the silent message in his gaze. He had fully expected her to be back at his house.

His voice dropped and became slightly hoarse. "Kid, come here."

She almost went, but years of heeding a cautious nature prevailed. "I'll get the coffee," she whispered.

"Damned foot! Causes me more trouble." She opened one cabinet, then another, searching for the coffee, trying to ignore the wild beating of her heart.

Suddenly two arms stretched out on either side of her to the counter, and she was hemmed in by Jared as he stood behind her. He moved close to kiss the nape of her neck and Courtney couldn't move. She closed her eyes while sparkling tingles fizzed within her from his light, brief kisses.

"Please, don't," she whispered.

"There isn't one damned good reason not to, and there are several fine reasons to go ahead," he murmured huskily between kisses.

If she turned, she would be lost, because his lips were only inches away. "There are more reasons to stop. I'll admit I'm vulnerable. And I'll admit . . ." She paused to take a deep breath. Her lungs seemed to have stopped functioning. She could feel his warm breath on her neck, could smell an enticing, woodsy scent. She tried to continue forcefully, but her voice wavered. "I'll admit your kisses are spectacular, but I don't want . . ."

" 'Tain't so, kid. You do want. With ninety-nine percent of your heart." His voice became velvet, a soft, furry touch that opened a door in the barriers around her heart. "Courtney." When he said her name, it sounded so special, so irresistible—and compelled her to turn around.

His arms slipped around her waist, pulling her to him as his head lowered. He kissed her, then raised his head slightly to whisper, "Put your arms around me."

She did. She couldn't fight the trembling that had seized her, the need to kiss him. She raised her face and parted her lips and forgot her inhibitions, her irritation, her caution.

Jared settled to kissing her with a thoroughness that made her temperature rise. She felt his fingers at the back of her head but didn't realize until he was through that he had unbraided her hair. It fell in soft golden waves over her shoulders and he ran his fingers through it.

"Oh, kid!" He breathed deeply, pausing a moment to look at her. Then his head lowered and again he took possession of her mouth and her senses.

He stroked her back, then his hand began to trail over her curves as if he would learn her entire body by touch instead of sight.

"Jared . . ." His name was a soft sigh, and the last word she said for so very long. She was like a boulder that had been poised on the edge of a cliff;

he had pushed her beyond a nebulous brink, and she couldn't stop the swirling fall.

Suddenly Jared picked her up and carried her to a chair. When he sat down with her on his lap, he groaned. She guessed he had hurt his foot by carrying her, but her senses were too overwhelmed for her to try to say anything about it. He framed her face with his hands and asked suddenly, "Kid, what the hell happened to you in that marriage?"

He waited while she gazed into his deep blue eyes. His voice was tender, and she felt as if she had found a friend she could talk to. She had told very few people about her marriage, but she felt she could tell Jared.

"My mother, my whole family sheltered me," she said. "My first contact with the world came when I went to college. I only went to town, to Nashville, but I lived on campus. During my sophomore year I met Mason and fell in love with him." She gazed out the window at the swirling snow, dredging up memories from long ago, things almost forgotten. "We were both young and immature. He was an only child from an old southern family, the same as I was. We fell in love and married." She turned from the window to look at Jared.

"Mason was so handsome, he was almost beautiful. He had coal black eyes, flawless bronze skin, white teeth, thick black hair. Girls worshiped him, and I felt fortunate. Everyone was in love with him—including Mason himself."

"What happened?"

She smoothed Jared's shirt collar, feeling the hard bone beneath the wool. "We might have had a chance, I don't know, if I hadn't gotten pregnant during our honeymoon. I took precautions, but I wasn't on the Pill. We had talked about waiting for children until we both were older." She touched the short dark hairs that curled at the open neck of his shirt, then moved her fingers back to his collar.

"Go on, Courtney."

"I was sick almost from the first day. So very sick. I think for a month or two Mason really tried to help, but he was young, handsome, and there were always adoring girls available."

Jared swore softly. She toyed with the top button of his shirt as she continued.

"Ryan was born in December. It was a cold, icy winter, and he was a sickly baby. He developed pneumonia and was in the hospital for quite a while. I wasn't too strong at the time. It became a nightmare. Mason felt hampered and tied down by Ryan. He didn't love Ryan. He didn't want him."

Jared swore again, louder this time. His finger stroked her cheek.

It was difficult to continue, but after a moment she said, "Finally, I had to leave him. It would have happened sooner or later. He had a girlfriend. Mason just didn't care about Ryan. It hurt so badly, each little way he rejected Ryan. He wasn't physically abusive, he simply didn't want his son."

"Damn."

She ran her fingers over the knee of her jeans, smoothing material that was already stretched tight. "Before we married, I was in love with Mason and I didn't see the flaws, didn't realize that when he kept putting off wanting children, he was hedging. He wasn't ready for the consuming responsibility of, as he said, 'a squalling, sticky brat.' "

Jared cursed in a flat, cold voice. "Does he live in Nashville?" he asked.

"No, thank heaven. He moved to California, and later his family moved there too. They were briefly interested in Ryan, but it faded. I don't know what Mason told them, but they became rather cold."

She glanced at Jared and saw his frown and a strange, bitter expression in his eyes.

"It's hell to grow up with a father that doesn't want you," he said. "I know because I've done it."

She felt a deep pang for Jared, for what might have happened to Ryan. She touched Jared's jaw tentatively. "I'm sorry," she said.

"Oh, hell. That's over."

"Ryan doesn't know, of course. I just explained that his father moved far away, that we couldn't get along."

"When he gets older, he may want more explanation."

"I know, but I can't ever tell him his own father didn't—"

"Shh, Courtney." He touched her lips with a tender finger. "I've heard enough to get the picture. Oh, kid, you're so soft, so caring. I know I'm gruff, but I don't mean much by it." His eyes focused intently on her. "Courtney, I need you. I like you. You have a warmth I need." He leaned forward slowly and lightly caressed her lips with his, pressed harder, then settled his mouth on hers with a hunger that made her heart pound.

And perhaps he had a strength that she needed. Jared was so many things she wasn't. Kent had been right; beneath his rough exterior, Jared was peaches and cream. He was sunshine and strength and understanding. She wound her arms around his neck to kiss him in return, and his arms tightened, crushing her to him.

Sometime in the next few minutes, he scooted off the chair, holding her, and they both lay down on the braided rug by the stove. The room smelled like roast; it was steamy and warm. Jared smelled like the woods on a spring day. Time lost significance as he caressed her slowly, waiting and building desire with deliberation. And each touch was a discovery, a heart-stopping, scalding encounter.

They lay together fully clothed while he loved her until she was trembling and aching with longing, until her fingers shook as she unfastened the buttons on his shirt. He peeled away her sweater and shoved aside the lacy bra to hold her full breasts, to kiss and tease and make her cry out.

She was aflame and twisted under him, thrusting her throbbing nipples against his solid chest. He was strong, bronzed, so perfect, and it seemed so right to have him hold her close. He pushed away her jeans, his hands caressing her slender legs.

She knew she could trust him, so she clung to him, raising her lips to his again. Gradually his fingers removed the last bits of clothing, and his kisses, the last hint of shyness. She lay in his arms, her curves and softness pressed to his angles and hardness, golden hair and ivory skin touching dark hair and bronzed flesh. She learned the textures of Jared's chest, with its mat of soft, curly hair that tickled so deliciously against her breasts. She touched and discovered his flat stomach, the heat of his maleness, his long, muscular legs.

He made love to her quietly, thoroughly, and earnestly, dallying to learn what brought a quick response, to banish her inhibitions, to find what drove her to moan softly with pleasure. For the first time she was with a man who gave to her completely, trying every way to please her, thinking only of her.

Once she caught his face and held him still while she asked, "Am I too prudish now?"

He kissed her palm. "Hell, no. I knew you wouldn't be."

He paused, his gaze penetrating to her soul. "Am I too gruff, too arrogant?"

"Ahh, you know the answer." She kissed his neck, trailing her lips to his ear.

She closed her eyes and tightened her arms around his neck. Later, poised above her, he suddenly stopped. "We fit together, you and I. More than this, more than physically. I need you, Courtney."

Her eyes flew open. She couldn't answer; she was drowning in his blue gaze. She slipped her hands across his powerful shoulders that had become important to her because they were Jared's.

"Courtney, you don't have to worry about protection. I'll take care." His leg moved between hers, shoving hers apart.

Dazzled, on fire, she trembled and kissed him, memorizing the feel of his fine body while she offered herself to him. His first thrust into her eager warmth made her gasp, then his slow strokes drove her to rapture, to a union that went deeper than physical joining. She cried out softly and clung to him as he shuddered and gasped, and said her name in a low, haunting tone that filled her with joy. Finally, he stretched out beside her, pulling her into his arms, and she closed her eyes, listening to his heart gradually slow to a normal beat. He stroked her hair, and his voice was a rumble. "Courtney?"

She twisted a dark curl of hair on his chest around her finger. She felt stunned and exhausted—and she still wanted him. She wanted to touch him, to stay close to him, to feel his arms around her.

He shifted and lay on his side, holding her close while he looked down at her. "I don't want to let you go."

"Thank goodness, I feel the same." She ran her fingers across his jaw, up into his hair.

He looked at her seriously as if he were debating something in his mind. She wanted to keep her own mind blank, to see only Jared. Not the Mr. Calhoun who had threatened Ebeneezer, but only the sensuous, thoughtful, exciting man she had been with for the past hour.

He caressed her legs, then his hand slid across her hip to her waist.

"I can't get enough of you," he said hoarsely.

"I feel the same way, except—"

"No." He placed his finger on her lips. "No 'excepts,' no intrusions. Not yet. Just let me hold you." They lay silent, entwined, as he stroked her hair and her back.

Courtney didn't know how much time had passed when she shifted and said, "I remember something about hot coffee . . ."

Jared chuckled and let her slip from his arms. She picked up her underthings, conscious of his steady gaze, and held her clothes in front of her. Blushing, she murmured she would be right back. She found the bathroom and showered quickly, then pulled on her clothes and returned to an empty kitchen. She was relieved that Jared was gone, yet the vacant room gave her a sense of loss. While she stood quietly, the white world of swirling snow she could see out the window lent a touch of unreality to the moment.

She found the coffee and coffeepot, started it, and began to grow more and more nervous over the change in her and Jared's relationship. Only half an hour ago it had seemed so perfect, so right to be in his arms. Now, after only minutes alone, questions rose to mind.

Then Jared filled the doorway and paused, his warm regard eliminating her nervousness and her questions. His hair was damp from a shower, and he was wearing a crisp khaki shirt that matched his pants. The shirt was open halfway down and the mat of dark hair tantalized her. He was sexy, appealing—a handsome man—but it was the expression on his face that took her breath away. His blue eyes were shining with pleasure, with an obvious joy because of her, her alone. She wanted to run and throw herself into his arms but an innate reserve held her back.

He crossed the room and wrapped his arms around her waist. She touched his cheek. "I feel like I've been hit by lightning," she said.

"I know what you mean, kid, but if you're honest, you'll admit there's been an attraction between us since the first moment we met." He grinned. "In spite of everything you've done."

"I've done!"

He laughed and said, "It's impossible to resist teasing—I know I'll get a reaction. Sparks fly from your big gray eyes. How about some lunch?"

"I know, cheese sandwiches and beer."

"Right, kid."

"Sit down and put your foot up. I'll get lunch. The coffee is ready."

While she sliced cheese, found the dishes, and opened his beer, she was conscious that Jared was watching her steadily. When she sat down across from him, she asked, "Want anything else?"

"Yeah, kid," he said softly, and she blushed.

He smiled and brushed her cheek with his knuckles. "You blush easily."

"I know. I can't stop it or I would."

"I like it. I can tell what's on your mind."

"That doesn't help."

The phone rang and Jared picked it up. She listened as he said yes and no and thanks, then she sat up alertly when he added, "I'll see Ryan Meade's mother and tell her. Fine. Thanks. Let us know when to expect them."

He replaced the phone, glanced past her out the window, then looked at her. "There's too much snow for the school bus to run. The kids will spend the night at school."

Her first thought was about Ryan. Her second was about herself. "They'll be fed and be warm enough?"

"Sure. For the kids it'll be a ball. Glad I'm not a teacher tonight."

She thought about Ryan staying at school with the others. She looked out the window at the tumbling snowflakes, and then she looked into Jared Calhoun's blue, blue eyes.

Ten

"You're snowed in here, kid," he said softly.

She swallowed. Her mouth felt as dry as cotton, her heart was thudding, her body was on fire. She would spend the night with him.

His voice dropped to a husky tone. "Let's go put on some records, build up the fire in the front room, and watch it snow."

"I'll do the dishes first."

"Forget them."

"I can't. It'll only take a minute."

He smiled. "Are you going to tidy up my life?"

Startled, she gazed at him. Without waiting for her answer, he said, "I'll get the fire going."

During the whole time she was cleaning the kitchen, her heart was racing, making her fingers tremble. She dropped a glass, cleaned up the broken pieces, splashed water on her blouse as she rinsed a dish, knocked over an empty bottle, and bumped into a kitchen chair.

"Kid, calm down," Jared drawled from the doorway. "You get any more nervous and you'll fly apart into little tiny pieces. I have a nice fire and two glasses of wine, and it's snowing to beat sixty. Want to play Scrabble? Watch it snow? Build a snowman?"

"I'd like to watch it snow."

He smiled, and she knew that was what he had hoped to hear. As she crossed the kitchen, he watched every step. A smoldering hunger in his eyes belied the earlier satisfaction. He wanted her and it showed plainly, and it sent her bloodstream into a heated froth.

He draped his arm across her shoulders, and they went into the front room where a fire was roaring, orange flames dancing up the chimney as the logs crackled and popped. Jared had pushed back the sofa and spread a thick brown comforter on the floor. Two glasses of red wine sat on the stone hearth.

"You were going to put on records," she said without paying attention to what she was saying. Instead she was concentrating on how she ached for him. Just thinking about his touch, his caresses, made her quiver and long for him, even as her cautious nature tried to subdue her heart. "Where are your records?" she asked.

"In the cabinet," he said. He lowered himself to the comforter and pulled her down beside him. She tucked her knees under her and turned to face him.

"I like it this way," he said, "quiet, only the sound of the fire. Outside it's snowing." He stretched his legs out, moving his injured foot carefully, his right hand resting on her knee. While his thumb traced circles on the inside of her leg, she glanced out the window at the great feathery flakes that swooped and dipped and tumbled earthward. Through the worn denim, his thumb felt as if it held an electric current that sent a constant flow of hot sparks into her system.

Jared handed her a glass of wine, raised his in a toast, and said, "Here's to Old Man Winter."

"Or Old Man Calhoun."

He chuckled, and she touched her glass to his, raising it slowly to her lips. She was held by his blue eyes as she sipped the wine. She was hot, but not from the fire. Her gaze was drawn to the open neck of his shirt, to the thick dark curls that were sensuous and soft, that covered his hard muscles. She longed to reach out, to touch his chest. Her gaze dropped to his legs, and she knew the strength in them, the coiled muscles beneath his tanned flesh.

He turned to gaze into the fire, a thoughtful look on his face. She sipped her red wine and wondered what he was thinking. When he looked back at her, she became aware of every nerve, of her golden hair falling over her shoulders, of the lack of makeup, the snug fit of her sweater and jeans, her bare feet—and she was as fully aware of Jared. Her breathing became shallow.

She took one more sip of wine, and her pulse rate climbed as he set his glass on the hearth, then took hers and placed it beside his.

He reached for her and she melted into his arms as naturally as a snowflake drifting to earth, returning his kiss to find the magic that spun between them.

Later, she opened her eyes and gazed out the window. She was lying in Jared's arms, her bare hip against his, her shoulder on his, their legs entwined. Mindlessly, she watched the falling snow. It was so easy to keep her mind blank, to enjoy the warmth of his body and the fire, to watch big feathery flakes swoop and hit the windowpane.

"Good-bye peppers and beer," he murmured softly.

It took a full minute before she realized what he'd said. She blinked, thought about it, then raised up on one arm to turn on her side, gazing down at him.

"No."

"Oh, hell. Here we go." His jaw set in a stubborn way, and he twirled a strand of silky golden hair around his wrist. "In spite of our differences, this is special." He sounded so solemn her heart jumped.

"There are too many complications, Jared. We have tonight; I can't think beyond that. We have Ryan and Guy to consider. An affair would be so involved. We have tonight."

"We have more than tonight, Courtney," he said gruffly in his commanding tone, and she laughed softly.

"Don't go all bristly. There are things I don't know about you."

"Ask away."

"I don't know where you were born—"

"Nashville, Tennessee, Davidson County." He drew invisible circles on her shoulder with a thumb. Tiny brushes that captured most of her attention. "You know what I have in my refrigerator," he went on, "what I wear, my sweet disposition, my black underwear, my scars—from the one on my shoulder to—"

"Enough of that!" She looked into the fire, watching the glowing embers. A log fell, sending orange sparks dancing up the chimney.

"Kid, I can see my beer going. My cigars have already gone. When a woman gets hold of your life, you lose control. I'll admit, albeit reluctantly, there are compensations."

"I don't have hold of your life, Jared." His name rolled softly off her lips, special to her now.

"Do tell. And what are we going to do about this?" He pulled her down and kissed her, a slow kiss that generated more heat than the burning logs and left her dazed. When she raised her head, he asked in a husky voice, "What about that? I'm going to hold you, kid. You're part of my life now. You and Ryan." His voice dropped to a fuzzy depth, and his blue eyes darkened. "We complement each other; we fit together, kid. As parents, as lovers."

His words stirred a sweet agony of longing within her to accept his declaration without hesitation or doubt. Parents, lovers—paradise.

"Let's shelve it for a while," he said, "and listen to the fire and snow."

Willing to do as he asked, she settled beside him. "You can't hear snow fall."

"Try."

She laughed softly. "I'll be quiet."

"Good, kid."

She lay quietly and mulled over what he'd said. His determination to keep her in his life made her heart drum. He was a sensitive, marvelous lover. He was a friend; he was good with Ryan. But beyond this one night that was so different in every way from all other nights—a record snow, the boys away, Jared beside her—she couldn't foresee the future. She glanced around the room, at the lumber stacked along one wall, at the tools, and fishing tackle.

She closed her eyes and tried to stop thinking. She snuggled closer to him, and his arm tightened to hold her as he turned on his side and slipped his leg over hers.

"Feels right, doesn't it?" he whispered.

She blinked, then answered honestly, "Yes, it does." It felt good to be held in his arms, to touch his angular, lean body that was pressed against her. She stroked his shoulder, then slipped her hand down his broad, muscular back and up again to wind her fingers in his soft, wavy hair. She closed her eyes and sighed.

The hours merged in a sensuous night of more lovemaking in front of the fire, a dream night that held no reality for Courtney except Jared's caresses, his kisses, and his strong body.

She woke in the morning to a bright sun glinting on the snow. She bathed, washed and dried her hair, then dressed in her sweater and jeans and went into the kitchen to find Jared frying two steaks. On the counter a pot of coffee perked noisily. When she looked at Jared, she felt the impact as if it were a blow to her midriff. A navy sweater and tight jeans revealed his whipcord leanness, and she remembered the feel of his chest and legs, his warm body. She shook her head as if to come out of a spell. "I'll cook the steaks," she said.

He glanced at her. "You sound breathless. Steaks get you all stirred up like that?"

"No. As a matter of fact, it was you."

Something flickered in his expression, changing as he put down a fork and wiped his hands on a towel. He crossed the room to her and placed his hands on her throat beneath her jaw, rubbing his thumbs lightly over her skin.

"How grand that sounded."

She could hardly get her breath. "It wasn't as difficult to admit as I thought. Maybe you're changing me."

"No. You're the same woman who jumped over a fence to save a hawk. Just a little more relaxed now."

His lips were inches away, almost on eye level and more enticing than breakfast. She ached to lean forward and brush them with hers.

As if he had the same impulse, he leaned down and kissed her until she pulled away to whisper, "Something's smoking."

"It's only my nerves." He kissed her again, and when they moved apart, he limped across the room to turn the steaks. A cloud of gray smoke rose from the pan and the steaks sizzled.

"You aren't using your crutch."

"Nope. My foot's better. I'm tough. Hope you like your steak well done."

"Have you ever eaten eggs or cereal?"

"Yep, that's why I eat steak now. After we eat I need to feed my horses."

"It's stopped snowing. Soon I can walk home."

"When the snow melts, I'll get the part for your Jeep and fix it."

"Thanks. Calhoun, you're becoming nice to have around."

He didn't smile, but looked at her with such intentness that her pulse jumped. "I hope you mean that with your whole heart."

"I do," she said, and the words came out breathlessly.

They ate, Courtney loaded the dishwasher, then they fed the horses, returning to the house to eat lunch and listen to the noon news and weather report. There was a segment about school kids who had been stranded overnight, but it wasn't Jefferson Davis Elementary, and the weatherman said warmer weather was on the way.

"Let's go make a snowman before the boys get home," Jared said. "Better yet, let's make a short-tailed snow dragon, then they can have fun adding a long tail."

Suddenly Courtney felt carefree. And how nice

his words sounded—"before the boys get home"
—as if they all belonged together. She pulled on her
jacket, then gazed in dismay at her feet and hands.
"I don't have the proper attire."

"One minute, please. Calhoun to the rescue."

He returned with a pair of Guy's boots, fur-lined
gloves, and a muffler, and they went outside into a
sparkling world to build a snow dragon.

Courtney gazed with wonder as Jared shaped
the head with icicle teeth. "You should do this for a
living, you know. You're quite good at it."

He grinned. "Calhoun—Snow Dragons, unlim-
ited. Melter of ice maidens in addition, huh?"

She laughed and threw a snowball at him, then
gasped when it knocked out one of the dragon's ice
teeth.

"I'm sorry."

Jared started toward her, and she jumped back.

"Now, look, it was only an icicle tooth," she said,
laughing and backing away from him. "Don't get
me wet!"

"Think you'll melt?" He reached out and caught
her, folding her into his arms.

Courtney yelped, expecting to be pushed down
into the snow. Instead, he smiled and gazed into
her eyes and everything changed.

His voice was soft as he said, "I love to hear you
laugh. You can knock out all his teeth and maybe a
few of mine if it makes you laugh that way." He
leaned forward and she raised her lips to his. The
kiss was rapturous and ended their work on the
dragon. Jared scooped her up, carrying her inside,
and this time their hands shook with eagerness.
They made love in Jared's big bed in the bright
sunlight that reflected off the snowy world outside.

When they went out again, it was early afternoon
and icicles dripped from the roof as the temperature rose. With zest Jared launched into work on

the head of the snow dragon while Courtney tack-
led the lower part.

"I've never seen an all-white dragon," she said
when she stepped back to survey their efforts.

Jared studied it, squinting. "I'll be right back."
He went inside and returned shortly with his arms
full of odds and ends: two chocolate cookies for
eyes, a long purple muffler to tie around the dragon's neck, and green food coloring for spots.

"A polka-dotted, grinning snow dragon by Jared
Calhoun! I wouldn't have believed it possible!"
Courtney laughed.

He winked, draping the ends of the purple muffler over the white neck, and threw his arm casually over the neck and posed beside the dragon.
"How do we look?"

"Icy and fierce!"

"Who, me? Fierce? Give us a kiss and we'll melt."

She proved him a liar, then said, "And now, kind
sir, I think I better walk home. I need to make sure
there's enough birdseed out."

"Let's go inside and warm up, have a cup of coffee, and then I'll go with you."

"Won't it hurt your foot?"

"Kid, it'll be worth it," he answered with such
force, she didn't argue.

So they drank coffee and afterward walked
through glistening snow and dark brown trees and
open fields, climbing the fence that separated their
property. At Courtney's house, Jared paused.
"What's wrong with your plumbing?"

"I have a leaky pipe."

"Let me look at it."

During the hour she was gone to put birdseed in
the feeders, Jared fixed the pipe and looked at the
furnace.

When she returned, he said, "You need a new
humidifier. I think you'll have to send off for it, but

let me check and see if I can get one. When Ryan gets home, if it isn't too late, tell him to come over and see the dragon. I'll drive him home later. Now, kid, kiss me good-bye."

She did and it turned into a long farewell, but finally he trudged across the snow toward his house. He turned to wave at her and she pressed her nose against the cold kitchen window and waved back.

"Bye, Jared," she whispered, and felt a loss. How silent and empty the house seemed without his presence.

The snow melted, Jared fixed her Jeep, and during the week Ryan went next door daily. The four ate together each night, usually at Courtney's. When the school carnival came, they went together, and Courtney knew the emotional ties to Jared were growing stronger. The four of them, parents and sons, were doing more and more things together. At the same time, her and Jared's snowy interlude of lovemaking had fanned desire. She longed to lie in his arms again, to kiss his flesh, to feel his hands on her. The slightest contact between them ignited a scorching flame that made her want more.

One afternoon he appeared at her house at two o'clock, just before a group from the Ornithological Society was due. When she told him that, he leaned against the fender of his truck and swore.

"Dammit, I never get you alone. Between the P.T.A., the school carnival, your bird tours, my horses, and the boys, we can't get a minute to ourselves."

"We have a date Saturday night."

"And I can't wait. Dammit!" The hum of a motor could be heard.

"Here comes my group."

"One quick kiss, kid." He reached for her, but the car came into sight, and he dropped his arms to his side. A flicker of disappointment stirred within Courtney. She was aching to feel Jared's arms around her, to have his kiss. It had been too long since they were alone!

Finally, the weekend came. The seventeenth of March now, the weather matched Courtney's spirits with a hint of early spring in Tennessee. The sunshine was warm, the sky blue, and robins flitted through the trees. She hummed a tune as she dressed in clinging black, changed her mind, and pulled on a soft beige woolen dress. She pinned her hair in a bun on top of her head, leaving tendrils curling over ears. The phone rang, and she picked up the receiver and said hello.

"Hey, kid," Jared said. "We've got trouble. My brother Lonnie called and they're in an uproar. Teddy, their six-year-old, fell off the garage roof."

"How terrible!"

"Yeah, he'll be all right. He landed in shrubbery. They're at the emergency room and they're in no condition to keep Guy tonight."

"Of course not. Just bring him over here. Mrs. Bartlett won't mind and Ryan will be glad to have company."

"You're sure?"

"Very."

"I won't argue with that. I can't wait. I feel like a kid on my first date."

"Is that what's the matter with me? I've changed clothes twice."

"Oh, kid! I'll be there in twenty minutes. I have our reservations at the Stratford Inn, and I'm looking forward to every second with you."

"The Stratford Inn. That is nice!"

"See you, kid."

After saying good-bye, she hung up and went to

tell Ryan that Guy was coming. As she finished dressing, the phone rang again. This time it was Mrs. Bartlett to tell Courtney she was coming down with something and would be too ill to stay with Ryan.

Courtney replaced the receiver, thought about the evening that would have been, then picked up the phone to break the news to Jared. As she listened to the phone ringing she decided he must have already left home, so she went to the living room to wait for him. When she heard him cross the porch, she went to the door, taking one last look down at her beige dress.

She opened the door to face Jared and Guy, and her heart jumped. She was barely aware of motioning Guy into the house, of telling him that Ryan was in his room. Her full attention was on Jared.

He was clean-shaven, his unruly dark brown hair combed. He was wearing a charcoal suit, a white shirt with a dark tie, and he looked so handsome she was speechless. It occurred to her after a few seconds that he seemed to be just as overwhelmed with her appearance. His dark lashes lowered as his gaze traveled over her breasts, her hips, down her long legs to her high-heeled pumps, and every nerve responded as if his fingers had drifted down her body.

"Courtney, how lovely you look."

"Thank you," she said softly, wanting badly to reach for him, yet standing, waiting.

"Where's your coat?"

"My coat? Oh! I have bad news. I tried to catch you before you left home, but Mrs. Bartlett is sick."

"Well, dammit to hell."

"I'll cook something. Come in and close the door."

"Oh, no. We've had enough of our home cooking. Yours and mine. We'll take the boys with us."

"To the Stratford Inn on Saturday night?"

"We'll try. Guy, Ryan!" he called.

Within seconds both boys came running down the hall.

"Get your hands washed, fellows. We're going out to eat. Tuck in those shirttails."

"Yes, sir!" Ryan said while Guy asked, "McDonald's?"

"No, the Stratford."

Guy groaned and trailed down the hall after Ryan. "I ate there once. It's quiet and dull."

Courtney smiled. "I can see we're off to a great start."

Jared touched her shoulder. "We are," he said huskily. "Don't let appearances fool you. I'm having a wonderful time."

The boys returned, pulling on jackets as they came. "Think they'll let two boys in jeans into the restaurant?" Courtney asked.

"Sure. The lady in the beige dress will so dazzle them, there'll be no problem."

"Who's the lady in the beige dress?" Guy asked, and Courtney laughed as they stepped outside.

"Mrs. Meade, Guy."

"Oh." He glanced at Ryan and twirled his finger in a circle near his head.

They climbed into the car, and Courtney's excitement returned full force. She didn't mind bringing the boys. The evening promised perfection.

As they drove down West End Avenue, Guy said, "There's a McDonald's, Dad."

"Yep, I see it."

In a few more minutes, Guy said, "There's a Showbiz Pizza, Dad."

"Guy, we're going to the Stratford."

Silence enveloped the backseat until they arrived

at the restaurant. One look at the bar filled with people, the crowd in the foyer, and Courtney knew they would eat elsewhere. Jared talked to the maître d' a moment, and then returned.

"Since it's Saturday night and our reservations are for two and now there are four of us, and they have such a crowd, we'll have quite a wait."

Courtney and Jared looked at the boys, who were standing quietly with long faces. Jared put his arm around her. "How about a pizza?"

"I'd love it."

"C'mon, guys. Off to eat pizza."

"Whoopee! Pizza!" Guy yelled, causing heads to turn. Courtney and Jared made a hasty exit, and the four drove to a pizza place.

The moment they stepped through the door of the restaurant, Courtney was assailed with sound. The front room was filled with video games. Behind it was a large room with a stage. Performing onstage was a band of animal puppets beating out a popular tune and drowning out everything else. A seven-foot stuffed orangutan strummed a bass fiddle. A gorilla played the drums, while a stuffed crocodile blew on a trumpet as colored lights flashed on and off. Surrounded by the din, families ate pizza at round tables.

They ordered, took a number, and Jared gave the boys money to play the video games. He and Courtney sat down, and he reached across the table to take her hand. They both laughed. The music prohibited ordinary conversation, so all they could do was shout and hold hands.

"This isn't what I planned," Jared said loudly.

"It's nice. I don't mind." She didn't because she enjoyed looking into deep blue eyes and watching a smile that made her want to hum.

The song ended and there was a momentary lull. Jared leaned forward to cup her face in his hands.

"Kid, I've always known what I've wanted, whether it's a car, a house, a horse . . ." His voice trailed off, and her pulse jumped and skittered.

"Courtney, will you—" The music started with a blare.

"Will I what?" she shouted.

"Marry me!"

Stunned, she wondered if she'd heard correctly.

"What did you say?" she shouted.

He scowled and yelled louder. "Will you marry me?" Several people turned to look at them, but Courtney didn't care. She was blissful. While it was a surprise, she, too, knew what she wanted. Badly. Jared cared about Ryan, about Guy. Beneath the bristly exterior he was sensitive and warm and strong. She needed him and she knew she was in love with him. And she suspected Ryan was growing to love Jared too.

A drum thumped loudly as she took hold of Jared's wrist and brought his hand around to kiss his palm.

"Yes, oh, yes."

"What did you say, dammit!" He glared at the stage.

"I said yes!" she shouted. He laughed and stood, pulling her up with him to kiss her.

She returned the kiss briefly, then sat down and blushed as a bunch of giggling teenagers at the next table put their heads together to talk and stare. The noise from the puppets was deafening, but she didn't notice. Her attention was enveloped in deep blue eyes. Jared reached across the table to take her hand again.

"There are so many things to settle, Jared," she said. "The boys . . ."

"Can't hear you!"

"There are so many things to work out!"

"Courtney. . . ."

"What? I'm sorry, I can't hear you."

A couple started to pass their table, then the blond woman stopped, her eyes growing round as she shouted, "Jared Calhoun!"

He stood up. "Hi, Trudy, Rob." He shook hands with the man.

"Land's sakes, Jared!" Trudy looked at Courtney.

"Courtney, this is Trudy and Rob Young. This is my neighbor, Courtney Meade."

Courtney stood up because the noise was too loud to carry on a conversation while seated. "You look shocked to meet me," she said, smiling because Trudy's mouth hadn't closed.

Trudy blinked, then looked at Jared and poked his shoulder with her finger. "Well, I am! Jared Calhoun, I wouldn't have guessed in a million years . . ." She blinked and suddenly Courtney wondered if Jared had some dark past he hadn't told her about. Trudy was definitely in shock. Courtney's curiosity ended when Trudy turned back to her and shouted, "Jared told me he was going to take you out, that he wanted the finest dining place in Nashville to impress you. I think Rob and I need to tell the man a few facts about impressing a woman."

Relief and amusement poured over Courtney. She saw the twinkle surface in Jared's eyes as she smiled and glanced around. "Trudy, this is the most romantic restaurant I've been to in my whole life."

"It is?"

"Damned odd taste, if this is what—" Rob started to say, but Trudy punched him with her elbow.

"I think it's wonderful," Courtney added.

"See, Trudy, I knew my lady would love it," Jared said.

My lady. Courtney's smile widened, and Jared took her hand.

"I think you two were meant for each other!" Trudy shouted.

"I think so too!" Jared shouted back. "I just asked her to marry me!"

"You what? Here, in this place?" Trudy looked at Courtney. "Hon, give it some thought. Don't say no too fast. I've worked with him for five years. He has some sense. I knew he didn't care for fancy living, but this . . . Rob and I just came to pick up our grandson. I can't wait to get out."

"I gave it some thought—and said yes," Courtney shouted.

Trudy looked intently at Jared. "Congratulations! No wonder all my matchmaking was useless. I didn't know what you really liked." She waved her hand in the direction of the stage. Jared grinned and squeezed Courtney's hand.

"Best wishes, folks," Rob shouted. "Trudy, my head's splitting, and I've lost sight of Terry again."

"Just a minute, Rob. When's the wedding?"

Courtney and Jared looked at each other blankly. Jared said, "Soon."

"Well, that beats all! Glad to see it. He's a nice guy. Don't pay any attention to his swearing."

Courtney grinned. "I won't."

"Bye, now. See you two again."

Jared pulled her into his arms for a quick hug. Courtney blushed and pushed away. "Don't, in front of all these children! You'll embarrass me."

He thrust his hand into his pocket and pulled out a small velvet box. He motioned for her to give him her hand.

She watched breathlessly while he opened the box. He removed the narrow gold wedding band from her finger. In its place he slipped a sparkling diamond. And this time she hugged him.

"Let's go tell the boys," he shouted.

"You think we should—"

"Can't hear you! Let's tell them."

When they moved away from the stage, they could talk without shouting. "Maybe we should get everything settled first, and then tell them," Courtney said.

"I can't contain myself! They'll adjust."

"Maybe not to this."

"They'll have to. The love we feel will spill over and cover them."

She saw the happiness in his eyes and felt as if she would glow in the reflection. "So much for wisdom!" she said, and he laughed as they went to hunt for their sons.

In the video room it was a decibel quieter, but the noise of electronic wizards, spaceships, monsters, and rockets prohibited normal conversation.

Jared took Guy to a corner while Courtney asked Ryan to go with her outside for a moment. They pulled on their coats and stepped into the quiet darkness. The lot was illuminated by red neon. Cars zipped past in the street with their headlights shining brightly in the night. Courtney sat down on a log in front of an empty flower bed. "Ryan, I want to talk to you."

"Yes, ma'am."

"Do you like Mr. Calhoun?"

"Yep."

"I mean really like him?"

"Yes, ma'am. He's not so scary after all, 'cept when he's mad."

"Has he been angry with you?"

"Nope. He got mad at Guy the other day when Guy pushed me."

"I didn't know that."

"He just told Guy to cut it out. It was okay."

"What did he say to you?"

"Nothing to me, 'cept something about don't take any guff. Didn't make much sense."

"Ryan, Mr. Calhoun's asked me to marry him."

"Gee whiz." Ryan's eyes grew round as he looked at her. She wanted to throw her arms around him and hold him, but she waited quietly to see his reaction.

"Are you gonna marry him?"

"I'd like to, but it'll change your life too."

"Gee. I'll live with Guy."

"Is that good or bad?"

"Sometimes it'll be good and sometimes it'll be bad, probably."

"Oh, Ryan, I want you to be happy!" She hugged him tightly.

"Hey, Mom!" She released him, and he asked, "Where'll we live?"

Courtney blinked and wished she had been more forceful in arguing with Jared to wait until they had everything settled. "I don't know," she said. "We have to work out the details. The main thing is, do you want me to marry him?"

While he thought it over, she held her breath. "Yeah, that might be okay. Do you love him, Mom?"

"I do, honey."

"Then I guess it's okay. You always said love's what's important. I'll have my own room, won't I?"

"Of course! I promise you that."

He looked relieved. "Guy's okay, but I don't want him into all my stuff. Are we gonna leave home?"

"I don't know. We'll have to make a lot of decisions." She thought of Jared's house, his peppers and beer, and realized a mountain of decisions lay ahead.

"Well, I'd rather live at our house. Guy never can find his things."

"I know. So would I. See my ring, Ryan."

With short, freckled fingers he turned the diamond, and she watched a rainbow glitter in its depth.

"It's pretty, Mom." He reached into his pocket. "Look what I won playing Pac-Man!" He held out a silver coin that was good for another electronic game.

Courtney smiled. "Shall we go inside?"

"Yes, ma'am. Guy's gonna show me how to play Frogger."

An hour later the boys were subdued and quiet as they drove home. When Jared turned the car onto the dirt road from the main highway, Courtney glanced back to see two sleeping children.

"I think you and I need to sit down and talk soon," she said.

"Whatever you say. I wish I had you all to myself right now."

She quivered and placed her hand on his knee, feeling the hard bone through the soft wool of his trousers. Her breathing altered and became difficult.

"What's bothering you, kid?"

"Two or three things. Your knee. Our houses."

"Courtney, I may have a wreck."

"My family has owned that house forever."

"You don't have to give it up."

"You'll move there?"

"Well, that wasn't what I had in mind. Keep it for Ryan or . . ."

"Or?"

He turned down her lane, slowed, and stopped, leaving the motor running while he glanced in the back at the sleeping boys. He touched her ear as his voice lowered. "Or for your youngest child. Courtney, if you want a baby, this time your husband will adore it."

She slipped her arms around his neck and raised her lips. When they moved apart, he sighed. "What an evening. I had so many plans . . ." He put the car in gear and continued up the drive.

"Jared, I'm not sure I can live in your house. It's so dark and full of lumber and tools and peppers."

"I knew it! There goes my life."

She blinked, then heard his chuckle as he touched her jaw with his knuckles.

"Sorry, kid, I can't resist teasing you. We'll redo my house. I'd rather avoid pink."

"It doesn't have to be pink, just nice and light."

"I'll get some paint tomorrow. What would you like?"

"Something cheerful."

"Red?"

"Oh, no! Maybe yellow." She envisioned a soft cream color, then glanced at him and forgot about houses and colors. A glow from the dash highlighted the sharp angles and contours of his face and she longed to touch him.

"What date can we set?" he asked. "Let's make it soon."

"Think of all the things we have to do! Paint, move furniture. We need to give the boys some time."

"Sure." He slowed and stopped the car near the back door. "I'll carry Ryan inside."

"He can walk."

"No, I'll bring him. You go in and turn down his bed."

She hurried through the darkness and pulled the covers back on Ryan's bed. It looked so natural, so right for Jared to carry the sleeping child inside. Together they got him undressed and tucked into bed, and then they tiptoed out.

"You better go. The car will be getting cold now."

"I know." He pulled her to him. "I can't believe my luck, kid."

"There are still things we don't know about each other. What church do you go to?"

"Methodist."

"Well, I'm Presbyterian."

"So I'll go to the Presbyterian church. They use the same book."

"Just like that?"

His voice became husky and he leaned close. "Just like that, kid. You came barreling across that fence into my life forever. I want you, Courtney. No casual relationship here. I want something strong and permanent."

She stood on tiptoe and closed her eyes. She forgot the questions as she kissed him and ran her hands down over his chest, across his narrow waist, over the bones of hips to his strong legs. He felt so marvelous; his words promised ecstasy.

She tingled and clung to him and wanted him to stay, but reluctantly they parted and she listened to him drive away.

Sunday afternoon Jared came to pick them up and the four went horseback riding. Later they ate a picnic dinner on the sanctuary grounds, then returned to Jared's until it was time for the boys to go to bed.

Monday morning Courtney heard the pickup pull into her drive and went outside to meet Jared. He stepped down from the truck. His foot had to be better, she thought, because he was walking toward her in a long, purposeful stride. His faded jeans molded his muscular legs, his short-sleeved knit shirt hugged his broad chest, and his blue eyes took the last bit of her breath when she faced him. Without a word he pulled her close for a kiss that only made her want more. Much more. Finally he raised his head.

"Good morning."

"Morning," she whispered, dazed.

"Are you alone, kid, or is some group on their way out?"

"You guessed it. Members of the Audubon Society are coming."

He groaned. "I would like a little private time with you. Do I have to make an appointment?"

"Maybe so."

"Courtney, I got the paint for the house. Come look at it." He draped his arm over her shoulders and led her to his pickup.

"You know, I think it's going to be difficult for me to talk to Guy about our marriage," she said.

"I hate to admit it, but sometimes it's easier for me to talk to Ryan than my own son. You've done a good job raising him."

She glowed in the best praise Jared could bestow. "Thank you. Ryan's easy to talk to, but I think that's just the difference in their personalities. And there's been only the two of us since he was a baby. That makes him have moments when he acts rather mature, and moments when he's a little boy again." While she talked, she was aware of Jared's hip brushing hers, his long legs, his arm warm across her shoulders. It had been so long since their night of love . . .

When they stopped at the side of the truck she saw that it was filled with cans of paint.

"You said you wanted it light and cheerful," he said while he set a can on the ground, hunkered down, and began to pry it open. "There, how's that?"

She gazed down at the thick yellow paint and didn't know what to say. He sounded pleased. The paint was cheerful. Very bright. And she suspected once it was all over the wall of a house, it would be even brighter.

"You don't like it."

He sounded so disappointed, she couldn't bear it. She smiled. "It's lovely."

"You mean that?"

"Yes."

"Will you move to my house?"

She took a deep breath. Before she could answer, he said, "Kid, look. Let's try my house. We'll keep yours, and if you don't like mine we'll try living here. Here, there, it really doesn't matter that much. I know you want to keep your home and the sanctuary."

He reached for her as the first car full of Audubon members came up the drive.

Jared groaned. "I think they do this on purpose."

She smiled. "No. This is just a good time of year for sighting birds. It's spring. And I didn't know I would be doing anything else, so I scheduled a lot of tours. I won't do that in the future."

"I want you in my arms."

Her heart thudded. "I may faint."

"I'll catch you. Kid, how about the seventh of April."

"That's soon," she said breathlessly.

"Tomorrow would suit me."

"The seventh is fine."

"Then I better paint fast."

"Morning, Mrs. Meade," someone called.

Jared capped up the paint, set it in the truck, and said, "See you later, kid. I'll pick you and Ryan up for hamburgers at my house tonight. Okay?"

"Sure. Bye, Jared."

A week later she was frying chicken while Ryan did his homework.

"Ryan," she said, "we're going to move to Mr. Calhoun's house, and you'll have your own room."

"This was Grandma's house."

"We'll keep this house, and someday it'll be yours. If we don't like Mr. Calhoun's house, we'll all move in here."

"Hey, that's neat. We'll have two houses. Hot dog!"

She thought of something else and put the lid on the skillet, then sat down near Ryan. "There's something I want to talk to you about. I know Mr. Calhoun swears a lot, Ryan, but you mustn't."

"Oh, he's already told me that."

"He did?"

"Yeah." He turned a page in his notebook. "He said a bunch of stuff about how he knows you don't like swear words, that he shouldn't use them, and Guy and I better not because they're something 'fensive—"

"Offensive. It means it offends. I don't like it."

"Yeah, and he said I'll be in hot water with him if I do and he's trying to reform and say 'phooey and drat' the way you do." Ryan rolled his eyes. "I don't think he's really trying hard. You should've heard him when the horse stepped on his hat."

"Oh, Ryan. You just mustn't repeat those words. You know I don't approve."

"Don't worry, Mom. You won't hear me say them."

"Guy doesn't talk much about the wedding."

"I think he's scared he'll lose his dad."

"Lose him?"

Ryan laid his pencil down and looked at her, a frown on his brow, and she was startled to glimpse the fear in his eyes. She reached out, and Ryan flung himself into her arms and clung to her.

"If you love Mr. Calhoun, Mom, will you still love me?"

"Oh, Ryan! Of course, I will! If you love Eben-eezer, it doesn't mean you stopped loving me any. Love isn't something rationed out like water and you only have so much to use. Sometimes I think the more you give, the more you have. I'll love you the way I always have, and now Mr. Calhoun will love you too."

He pulled away and blushed, sitting down again. "I don't think Guy's gonna love me."

She laughed. "You'll get along."

"We'll be brothers?"

"Stepbrothers."

"That's kinda neat."

"How's the paint job coming?" she asked, getting up to turn the chicken. "I haven't been over there this week."

"It's yellow, Mom. I mean yellow-yellow. It's like my old plastic raincoat. The kids on the school bus can see the yellow through the trees from the road. It's almost as bright as the bus. The kids asked Guy if he lived in a school bus."

"Oh, dear. Mr. Calhoun is trying, Ryan, so let's not hurt his feelings."

"I know. I told him it was super, but it's really yel-low. He wears sunglasses all the time so maybe he can't tell."

"Well, we'll just be nice about it," she said, turning over the bubbly, golden chicken, her thoughts on Jared.

The next evening Jared came by to pick them up for dinner at his house. While Guy and Ryan played with two Rubik's Cubes in the backseat of the Ford sedan, Courtney peered through the windshield, her curiosity mounting about the house as she glimpsed flashes of bright yellow through the trees.

The boys dropped the cubes to sit up and see

how impressed she would be. "We're almost there," Guy said. "Dad and I've painted every day."

"You're a big help, Guy," Jared said. "And we're halfway through. Wait until you get a full view, kid. I think you'll agree that it's bright and cheerful."

"Maybe you ought to loan her your sunglasses," Ryan suggested.

"Why?"

"Gives a nice tint to it. Horace Wakefield told about it in his language arts report, and Miss Creighton wants to come out and take a look."

"Well, it's not that unusual," Jared said. "It's just a cheerful yellow house."

"Bright and cheerful," Ryan said. "Get ready, Mom."

They drove around a curve, and she had a full view of Jared's yellow house—and she went into shock. The sprawling house was blinding in the late afternoon sunshine. She stared at it, realizing it represented Jared Calhoun's efforts to please her. She glanced at him and he winked while the two boys hung over the seat to see her reaction. Ryan giggled.

"What'cha think, Mrs. Meade?"

"Yeah, kid, what do you think?"

"It's so cheerful." She couldn't look at Ryan.

"Kind of unforgettable, isn't it, Mom?"

"Ryan, don't you like it?" Jared asked.

"Yes, sir! I think it's neat. I like Guy's suggestions to put polka dots on it."

"Oh, no!" Courtney found her voice. "No, it's fine just the way it is now."

"You really think so?" Jared asked.

"I think so," she said cautiously.

Jared parked, held the door for her, and led her inside. The living room had been painted white, changing it entirely. It was light and neat. Books were neatly stacked on the brown oak bookshelves.

The tools, the magazines and papers, the lumber and fishing tackle, were gone.

"It's nice," she said, overwhelmed that he had tried so hard to make her happy.

"We'll move your furniture tomorrow. We'll finish when we get back from our honeymoon."

"Our honeymo—"

His kiss stopped her words. He pulled away and said, "Now, there's something else." He took her arm and walked swiftly to the kitchen to throw open the pantry. She gazed at enough miscellaneous items to stock a small grocery. Then he held open the refrigerator.

An assortment of items filled the shelves. At the back she spotted two bottles of beer and a jar of peppers, but there were also jars of mayonnaise, mustard, pickle relish, a head of lettuce, bottles of milk, most of the things she kept at home.

"See, there's milk and orange juice and all sorts of weird food like that."

She laughed. "Weird food! You can keep your peppers and beer, but I think Guy should drink something besides soda pop."

"You win on that one, kid."

She turned, and his bedroom blue eyes stopped her thought processes.

"One more week, Courtney, and you're mine forever."

She wound her fingers in his hair. "The house is a little too yellow, isn't it?" he said. "I guessed that from Ryan's subtle hints. We can have painters redo it when we get back."

"No." She gazed into his eyes and said firmly, "No, I love it. This bright yellow house would never belong to someone prudish and prim, an icicle . . ."

"Hottest icicle this side of the Pole," he said in a deep voice.

"I love it bright yellow. You can let Guy put pink polka dots on it if you want."

Laughing, he hugged her and started to kiss her, but was interrupted by the boys.

"When's dinner, Dad?" Guy asked.

"Soon. We'll call you."

They vanished out the back door, and Jared reluctantly stepped back from Courtney to pull a roast out of the oven.

"What can I do?" she asked.

"Everything's done. Just sit down."

"I talked to Ryan yesterday. He said Guy's afraid he'll lose you."

Jared paused, setting the steaming roast on top of the stove. "Lose me! That's damned nonsense! I've talked to him and everything seems fine."

"Does it really?"

"Well, sometimes he's a little cross, but it'll pass after we're married. It'll be better for him to have you around."

"I hope so," she said, watching the boys through the window and praying silently that Jared was right.

It was spring in Tennessee and the weather was perfect. Yellow forsythia, red tulips, and yellow jonquils were blooming in the greening yard. The sky was blue and clear, and the sun warmed the air.

What wasn't perfect was Courtney's stomach. She tried to ignore its nervous flutters as she brushed her hair, twisting it and fastening it in a roll on top of her head. She smoothed the pale blue silk dress with its short sleeves and straight skirt. At her throat was a necklace of pearls Jared had given her the night before, and pinned on her dress was a white orchid, also from Jared. She felt jittery and wondered for the hundredth time if Ryan and Guy would get along while she and Jared

were away on their honeymoon. Mrs. Bartlett wa
going to stay with the boys. She was in Courtney'
room now to get last-minute instructions, an
Georgia, Courtney's best friend, was sitting by th
window, smoking and staring outside.

"Jared is so nice, Courtney," Mrs. Bartlett said
adjusting her bifocals. "I just wish your parent
and grandmother could be here. It would mak
them happy to see you married to such a nice
handsome young man."

The description was stupefying. Courtney ha
never once thought of Jared Calhoun in suc
terms as "a nice young man." "Thank you, Mrs
Bartlett." Courtney glanced at her watch. "It
almost time." She hadn't seen Jared all day. Sh
didn't know where they were going on their honey
moon, but she suspected Ryan and Georgia knew

She glanced at Georgia, who was stretching, th
sunshine catching deep red glints in her aubur
curls.

"I saw the groom arrive. He's a doll. I'll trad
places with you, Courtney. He's very masculine—
and very sexy."

Courtney smiled. "He is at that. I hope Ryan'
happy."

"Ryan? He's a kid. They adjust to anything.
Georgia glanced at her watch. "Time to go. Soo
you'll be Mrs. Calhoun." She stood up an
smoothed her cream-colored dress. "I wish you a
the happiness in the world. I think you'll have
with Jared."

"Thanks." Courtney opened the door an
stepped into the long hall that ran the length of th
house. At the front Reverend Thompson from th
Presbyterian church was standing beside Jare
and his brothers. Her heart jumped when she saw
Jared. Dressed in a dark suit and white shirt, h
looked so handsome! Her mouth went dry, and sh

orgot the others, the time, or what was happening. Down the full length of the hall she looked into his blue eyes, and the world vanished. If he opened his arms, she would walk right into them. She felt pulled toward him, wanting to touch him, to be near him.

"Courtney!" Georgia said.

"Oh, sorry."

Georgia smiled. "Don't blame you. He's gorgeous."

She walked slowly down the hall to Jared, and he took her arm. "Hi, kid."

She felt a flush of warmth and floated into the living room on his arm. Jared had sent flowers early in the morning, and white and pink carnations were banked on both sides of the fireplace where the ceremony would take place. The windows to the porch were open, letting in fresh air. Jared's relatives were present, along with her friends. Reverend Thompson waited.

"Where are the boys?" she asked suddenly.

Eleven

Reverend Thompson smiled, opened his mouth, but before he could speak, voices came from the direction of the front porch.

"You stink!"

"Oh, yeah! You leave me alone, Guy Calhoun."

"Oh, no!" Courtney gasped.

"You leave me alone! Don't go near my stuff."

"You're the one who's in my stuff! Gimme back my model."

"I worked on it too, so buzz off!"

"You can't go into my room!"

"You can't live in my house!"

"Dammit to hell," Jared breathed, and turned to look out the front window. "Just a minute, Reverend."

"I won't!" Ryan said.

"Twit! Your mom chased my dad and made him marry her!"

"Oh, no!" Courtney turned to the door. Jared

was already striding through it, and Mrs. Bartlett was standing at the front window. "Ryan!" she called. "Boys, please stop."

"I thought they were right here beside me!" Sandra Calhoun, Jared's sister-in-law, exclaimed.

Courtney ran outside after Jared as the boys tumbled off the porch, smashing jonquils as they rolled in the dirt.

Ryan pinned Guy to the ground, gripping the bigger boy's shoulders and banging his head up and down in the dirt. Both of them were yelling unintelligible names at each other, but Courtney caught Ryan's, "Take it back, Guy! Take it back!" and Guy's "Twit! You can't ride my horse again!"

Jared jumped off the porch and pulled the boys apart. "Guy!" he thundered, and everyone froze.

Courtney blinked, holding her breath, afraid for an instant that Jared would strike Guy. Both boys were cut and dirty. Blood was running from Guy's nose and split lip and from Ryan's nose and skinned cheek.

Jared swore. "Dammit, Guy!"

Guy wilted, putting his face in his hands and sobbing. Courtney suddenly felt sorry for both males, but she had a more immediate concern in Ryan, who was sobbing as loudly as Guy. She started across the porch.

"Courtney," Georgia said from behind, and touched Courtney's elbow.

She whirled around. "Georgia, please. We'll just have to wait. Tell Reverend Thompson."

"Hey, now wait a minute, Courtney," Jared began, but she interrupted him.

"We have to straighten this out." If she had to look at the two bleeding faces much longer, she might faint. "Maybe we rushed things."

"Now, look, kid, that wasn't me—it was my son. He's just a kid."

"Ryan, I want to talk to you," she said. "Go to your room." Sobbing, he ran inside.

"Your son needs you," she added to Jared. "And mine needs me." She marched into the house. Behind her she heard Guy Calhoun wailing, "Dad . . ."

She walked past the astonished guests and went to Ryan's room, her lips tightly compressed.

Ryan was lying on his bed crying, and she crossed the room to take his arm. "Come here and let's clean up your face."

"I hate him!"

"Ryan!"

"I do! Are you gonna get married?"

"Not now," she answered, and wondered what she had said to Georgia. She had been distraught at the time, and now she could only recall Georgia touching her arm, asking something about Reverend Thompson.

"I hate Guy Calhoun."

"You don't." She went to the bathroom, rinsed a washcloth with cold water, returned to Ryan, and knelt down in front of him. "Since February you and Guy have been together constantly. That isn't hate."

"My nose hurts. And I'll bet his does too."

"Will you stop?"

She wanted to cry too. She sponged off his face gently. Ryan flinched. "He's the twit!"

"Shh, that's enough! You know I don't approve of fighting. You didn't solve one thing by doing it, did you?"

"Ummm."

"Did you, Ryan?"

"No, ma'am, but he said some bad things. And he came in my room and took my model."

"There's a way to settle things without using your fists, and you might as well learn how now."

She dabbed at his cheek and wondered if Jared was having the same conversation with Guy.

While she continued cleaning Ryan's face, she heard voices approaching, the low tone of Jared's voice, then a knock on her door.

"Kid . . ."

"Just a minute, Ryan. I'll be right back." She went to the door and opened it. Bracing herself, she faced Jared. He had pulled off his coat, rolled up his shirtsleeves, loosened his tie, and his broad chest looked like a bulwark of strength. She wanted to fling herself into his arms. She thought of the boys and said, "I think we rushed things."

"They're only kids. They blew a fuse today, but it doesn't have to become a habit. I'll take Guy home, clean him up. The others have gone."

It shouldn't be this way, she thought. They should be married now. She nodded, afraid her voice would waver. Jared's dark brows were drawn together and he looked as miserable and annoyed as she felt.

"We'll go now. I'll call after a while," he said.

"All right." She watched him go and wanted him to stay. "Jared . . ."

He turned. His eyes narrowed and her words faded. He needed to talk to Guy. The minister, Jared's family, her friends had gone. She shook her head. "I'll be here."

"Yeah, kid."

Her throat tightened and she went back to the bathroom with Ryan.

"Mom, my nose is still bleeding and my eye hurts."

"Ryan, this is so dreadful. Next time, think before you hit someone."

"You're not getting married because of me."

"It isn't just you. I hope you and Guy learned something. Use your head instead of your hands."

"Yes, ma'am. I'm sorry."

"Oh, Ryan!"

They talked a few more minutes. Finally, she had done all she could for Ryan's injuries, said all she could say about his fight. And in the back of her mind awareness grew that time was passing and Jared hadn't called.

Had they made a mistake? She knew they hadn't. She loved Jared Calhoun, and they were good together, good for each other and for the boys.

She went to her room to sit by the window and stare outside. What would be best? Was Jared having a difficult time with Guy? She ran her finger along the sill, watched a robin in the flower bed, and stopped thinking. Late afternoon changed to dusk, and the more time that passed, the more certain she was that they could handle the problems, that she loved Jared and wanted a future with him. Suddenly, she stood up and began to move. She wasn't going to wait around for Mr. Jared Calhoun's call!

She changed into jeans, braided her hair, and called to Ryan. When she didn't get an answer, she went into his room. His suit lay on the bed, and she guessed he had changed and gone outside. She stepped to the back door, calling, "Ryan!"

There wasn't an answer. Somewhere in the distance, she heard a bird's cry. She wondered if he had gone to the Calhouns'. She scribbled a note to him in case he came back, climbed into the Jeep, and went next door.

When she drove up, Jared came out of the house, and the moment she saw him, her heart soared with joy. His long legs carried him quickly to her. Brown curls tumbled over his forehead. He was still wearing his dark slacks and white shirt, and looked as appealing as ever.

When he reached the Jeep, his arms went around her waist. He swung her out, crushing her in his embrace while she locked her arms around him.

"Courtney, we'll work the problems out together."

"I'm sorry I was so upset." They looked into each other's eyes and laughed. For the first time in hours, she began to feel happy.

"We'll try again tomorrow. I've talked to Guy. He felt terrible, but that doesn't do much for us now. All four of us should sit down together and discuss fighting."

She touched his throat, her fingers drifting along his jaw, across solid bone and skin that was faintly stubbly. "Jared, is Ryan here?"

"No. I haven't seen him."

"I can't find him." She frowned. "I thought he'd be here."

"I've been looking for Guy. I left him alone for a time, and when I went back to find him, he'd gone outside. That's why I didn't call you. By the time I called, you were on your way here, but I didn't know that."

And she saw a look in his eyes that told her he had been in agony wondering about her.

"Come on, kid. We'll look for them."

He put his arm around her waist, and they went to the barn, where he checked on his horses.

"The horses are all accounted for. Let's go back to the house." As they walked to the house gravel crunched beneath their feet. "Kid, this was to have been our wedding night," Jared said huskily, and her veins flowed with heat. A quiver shook her as she moved ahead of him into the kitchen.

The house was silent, then toenails scraped on the bare floor and Admiral appeared from the kitchen. Jared idly scratched the dog's head and turned on the lights.

"Sit down," he said. "I'll go look in Guy's room." He raised his voice. "Guy!"

"Jared, where would we have been tonight?"

He looked at her intently, and she felt a blush rise. In a deep voice, he said, "In bed."

She couldn't get her breath, but he turned and the spell ended. As he started out of the room, she said, "You know what I meant. Where were we going?"

"We'll be there tomorrow night. You'll have to wait and see."

He left and within minutes she heard swearing. He returned with a paper in his hand and a scowl on his face.

"Dammit, if it isn't one thing it's two." He pinned her with a fierce look. "Did you tell Ryan you wouldn't marry me?"

She squirmed uncomfortably. "Well, I was upset, and I meant not now, not today. Why?"

"I said as much to Guy."

"You did!"

"Yeah, kid." His face flushed. "Hell's bells! I meant today too! I want to marry you. I can't get along without you."

"Thanks. What's that have to do with the boys?"

"Well, now, kid, you're going to learn a lesson about men. You thought they hated each other and couldn't get along. Read this."

She took the paper and read the childish scrawl aloud:

"*Dad,*
"*Ryan and I are keeping you and Mrs. Meade from marrying. We didn't mean to so we're leaving. Don't worry about us becuz*

we're safe. We'll come home when your mar-ryed. Guy.

"Dear Mom,
"I'm going to. We want you and Mr. Cal-houn to get married. I love you. Ryan."

"Oh, my goodness!"

"I knew I should cover my ears," Jared drawled.

"What'll we do? It's night now. Where can they be?"

He ran his fingers through his hair. "They said they'd come back when we're married, so they can't be too far away or they wouldn't know whether we got married or not." He paused. "If they'll come back when we're married, the simplest thing to do is get married."

"Without your family?"

"Do you care?"

"I'd like for Ryan to be here."

"I'll call Reverend Thompson, you go home and change. When they see the reverend appear, they'll come back."

"I think I'm being railroaded by a couple of kids."

Jared grinned. "It's okay with me. Besides, I can't keep changing reservations and flights. I canceled everything this afternoon."

"You did? Well, you must—"

He waved his hand. "Keep your shirt on. I made them again for tomorrow. I planned to come over and try to change your mind."

"We could just look for them."

"This will be easier."

Suddenly she smiled. He walked over to her and held her, kissing her lightly. "I like that smile, kid."

"I better run." And after one long, passionate kiss, she did. As she slowed beside her house the headlights caught a figure running down the lane, and Ryan came into view. He was covered with mud and his hair hung in his eyes.

"Ryan!"

"Mom, come quick! A log rolled on Guy and he's smashed down and I can't get him out."

"Ryan, slow down. Where is he?"

"We're at the pond. We were gonna come home and get something to eat, and we were at the pond and he slipped and fell. A log rolled and came down on top of him and he can't get out from under it."

"I'll take the Jeep and go. You run inside, call Mr. Calhoun and tell him, then you come back in case I need your help."

"Yes, ma'am." He ran inside the house.

She hurried to the garage, found a tow chain and threw it into the Jeep, then started down the lane in the direction of the pond that was deep in the sanctuary.

When she arrived, at first she couldn't see Guy, but the moment she turned off the motor and silence descended, she heard him crying.

"Guy!"

"Help me! I can't get out! Dad!"

"I'm here, Guy," she called. She drove closer, spotted him pinned beneath a large log, and turned the Jeep so the headlights shed a circle of light on him. Her breath caught at the sight of him.

He was waving his arms back and forth, crying as he struggled. And with each movement, the log sank deeper in the mud, settling more heavily on top of him.

"It's all right, Guy. I'm here," she said, and knelt beside him.

"Help me!"

"Calm down, Guy!"

He stopped floundering and big blue eyes looked at her. "I want out."

"I know you do. I'll get you out. Does the log hurt you?"

"A little. I can't move."

She saw he was pushed down into the soft mud that had saved him from being crushed. "I'm going to back the Jeep up very close," she said, "put a chain around the log, and try to pull it off. Now, lie quietly. Will you?"

"Where's Dad?"

"He's coming. Ryan found me first."

"I want out." He started crying again.

"Guy!" Courtney was firm, but she placed her hand on his cheek. "Guy, mind me. Lie still. I'll get you out."

He stopped moving again, tears streaking his muddy cheeks as he lay panting. "You can?"

"Yes, but you have to help." She prayed she could while she talked in a calm voice. "Do just what I say."

"This is tight."

"It won't be in a minute." She ran to the Jeep, backed up carefully, then secured the chain to the bumper and around the log.

"It's getting heavy!" His voice was filled with panic, but he lay quietly watching her.

"Now, Guy, I'll go slowly. If it hurts you more or presses harder, call to me to stop."

She climbed into the Jeep and began to move forward slowly. The chain grew taut, pulled, and suddenly she wondered if the Jeep could move the big log. She eased her foot down on the accelerator. Nothing happened. Then the log shifted. It slid a few inches. She pressed her foot down a fraction more and the log slid another inch, then another.

Suddenly Guy yelled. "It's heavier! It's getting tighter on me!"

She climbed out to look. "Guy, don't wiggle. I'll find something to raise the log. A rock, something to raise one end so when I pull, it will be off of you enough—"

She heard a motor and looked up to see Jared's truck roaring down the lane.

"Here comes your father."

Jared was out in a second, Ryan following. Jared removed two stout boards from the truck and sprinted to her. "I started pulling the log," she said, "but then Guy said it was getting heavier."

"Get in and try again. Ryan, you come help, and we'll pry the log up while your mom pulls it. Guy, when I tell you to move, you try to scoot out."

As she started the Jeep again Jared and Ryan put boards beneath the log and threw their weight against them to raise it. In seconds Guy yelled, and she saw a blob of mud wriggle away from the ground.

Jared and Ryan dropped their boards and Jared called to her. "Stop! He's out!" He swung Guy up in his arms, hugging him and getting mud on his good clothes. They hurried to the Jeep and put him on the seat. Guy was crying as Jared asked, "Do you hurt anywhere?"

Guy wiped his cheeks with the back of his hand, smearing more mud over his face. "My shoulder and my side hurt a little. I slipped and fell. The log rolled off another one and fell down on top of me."

"We'll take you home. I ought to tan two hides, you know."

Both boys looked down.

"We didn't mean to stop you from marrying," Ryan said.

"You didn't, Ryan," Jared said. Suddenly Jared drew Courtney and Ryan close to the Jeep. He managed to put his arms around all of them, drawing them together. "We're going to be one family from now on."

Courtney looked into his blue eyes. He had mud

on his cheeks and jaw, down the front of his clothes, but he was the most handsome, adorable man she had ever seen. She smiled at Ryan.

"Ryan, Guy," Jared continued, "we'll have our own places in your lives. There won't be any more calling us Mr. and Mrs. Boys, what'll it be?"

"I dunno," Ryan said.

"Guy, how about calling Courtney, Mam? And, Ryan, how about calling me Pap?" He looked at Courtney. "Okay, kid?"

"Fine, if it's all right with the boys."

Both nodded solemnly.

"You two, you're getting off lightly. Do you know how much you worried us?"

"No, sir," each boy answered at once.

"Now, let's go to a wedding."

"Tonight?" Ryan asked.

"Yes. I suspect Reverend Thompson is waiting at your house. I called the relatives."

"You did?" Courtney asked.

"Sure. Guy and I'll go home, clean up, and get back as soon as possible."

They were married at ten o'clock at night and at eleven, they kissed the boys good-bye and went to the airport.

Lights in the airport parking lot shone clearly into the car. Courtney wanted to throw her arms around Jared. Instead, she asked, "Aren't you going to tell me where we're headed? After all, I'll know as soon as we go to the plane."

"Where would you like to go the most?"

"Suppose I say a place around the world from where we're going? Tell me."

"Answer my question, kid."

"I think . . . to bed."

His blue eyes changed, and he reached out to pull her into his arms and kiss her. Abruptly, he released her. "I'm not spending my wedding night in the parking lot at the airport. Where would you like to go most of all?"

"Any place will do."

"Kid . . ."

"Switzerland." She ran her finger across his lips, then to his jaw. She wanted to be alone with him. "I'd like to see the Alps. I want more to be alone with you."

"We'll be there in a week."

"We will?" She stared at him; she was in shock. "You really mean it! In a week? We're taking a boat?"

"Nope. Come on." He took her arm, locked the car, picked up their luggage, and they went to a small plane. When Jared helped her up and climbed behind the controls, she reached over to take his hands.

"Now, look! Are you flying to Switzerland? What is this? Is this your plane? You better tell me what's going on . . ."

"Here comes the bristly burr again. Kid, I have a home on the Gulf Coast. We'll fly down there for the next six days, then maybe we'll be ready to tour. We'll go to Switzerland then."

"You're kidding!"

"No. Ryan told me you always said you wanted to see Switzerland. The boys will join us next weekend."

"Oh, Jared! Switzerland!"

"Right now, I want you all to myself."

While her heart drummed with excitement, she settled back, and they flew to the coast, where they rented a car and drove to his home on a private stretch of beach.

By the time Jared had opened the door and carried her over the threshold, the first faint rays of the morning sun were visible, shedding a rosy glow above endless calm water.

Inside the house Jared held her while she glanced around at a rustic room with polished oak floors, cypress walls, and rattan furniture with bright green cushions.

"It's pretty."

"Sure is," he murmured as he set her on her feet.

"Jared . . ."

"Hmmm?"

"You wait right here, Mr. Calhoun." She picked up her suitcase and went into the bathroom and close the door.

Twenty minutes later she emerged with her skin glowing from a bath, her golden hair falling softly over her shoulders, and a gossamer black lace nightgown on.

Jared had pulled off his tie, unbuttoned the top button of his shirt, and poured champagne.

"This is one time, Jared Calhoun," she said, "when you're not going to call me 'kid.' "

He picked up the champagne and walked toward her while his gaze took in the sight of her. His look made her nerves sizzle. She reached for the champagne, brushed his fingers, and felt a jolt from the slight contact.

His voice dropped to the low husky level that made her pulse hum eagerly.

"Here's to a hawk named Ebeneezer—and to our future, Mrs. Calhoun."

Smiling, she sipped the bubbly champagne. Jared took her glass from her, placing in on the table beside his glass, then he straightened to look at her, a smile curling his mouth. "You're beautiful, kid."

She raised an eyebrow, placed her hand on her hip, took a deep breath, which made her breasts thrust against the filmy gown, and drawled "Calhoun, I'm not a kid."

Suddenly he looked so solemn her heart skipped He stepped forward to pull her to him, and when he spoke his voice was low and hoarse.

"Courtney, I love you."

Epilogue

Courtney heard a screech. She sat up in bed and looked out the window to see a small girl with yellow braids running from the corral toward the house. A large rooster flapped its wings and charged after her.

"Jared, that bird is after Ginger again! He'll hurt her . . ." She paused as a back door slammed and Ryan and Guy raced toward the corral.

From the pillow beside her came a muffled, "Did her rescuers just leave the house?"

"Yes, there they go. That rooster is downright mean."

"Won't be long. He'll probably be on the table for dinner soon."

"Ginger has three fathers, you know?"

"Hmmm. Kid, you talk too much for early in the morning."

"Oh, the boys are chasing the rooster now!"

"Kid—"

"Jared, maybe you should go see about it."

"Quiet, kid." An arm went around her waist, and she was pulled down against a bare, muscular chest. Bare legs wrapped around hers.

"Jared, I'm over thirty. Are you going to call me 'kid' when I'm forty?"

"Forty—fifty—you'll always be 'kid.' " He kissed her throat. A stubble covered his jaw and tickled her skin as he brushed against her shoulder. He pushed her gown away to fondle her breast, then took it in his mouth to tease and kiss her.

She gasped, winding her fingers in his hair. " . . . need to get up and cook breakfast . . . five hungry people . . . steaks and pepper sauce and eggs."

He kissed her throat, nuzzling her neck and trailing hot kisses to her ear while he stroked her legs and hip. "To hell with breakfast."

"I heard Ginger swearing yesterday and that's your fault!" she said breathlessly, clinging to his broad shoulders.

He raised his head and his eyes twinkled, soft brown curls shot with gray fell over his forehead. "I heard Guy say 'pish-tosh'—that's worse than Ginger swearing. Damnation, it makes him sound like a twerp." His lips drifted lower. "Only salvation was, none of the kids knew what he'd said. They thought it was newfangled swear words." He chuckled while he trailed his fingers lazily over the curve of her hip.

She gazed sleepily into bedroom blue eyes and pulled him down. "Calhoun, you're the greatest!"

"Kid, you're the sexiest broad on earth!"

THE EDITOR'S CORNER

With this month's books we begin our *third* year of publishing LOVESWEPT. And are we excited about it! It feels as though we've only just begun, and I hope our enthusiasm for the love stories coming up next year is matched by your enjoyment of them.

Publishers work far in advance of the dates books reach the public. Did you know that producing a LOVESWEPT romance takes the same amount of time as a baby? That's right, nine full months! Even as you are reading this we are sending to our Production Department the LOVESWEPTS for January *1986*. So, with great certainty, I can assure you that our third year will continue the tradition of emotional and exceptional romances you've come to expect from LOVESWEPT. I envy you. I wish I had all the great forthcoming LOVESWEPTS to enjoy for the first time. But, then, you should just see what delicious stuff is on my desk right now for 1986! Back to next month, now, and the "four pleasures" in store for you.

Marvelous Barbara Boswell is back with **DARLING OBSTACLES,** LOVESWEPT #95. The title refers to the seven children the heroine and hero (both widowed) have between them. Never have there been seven more rowdy or adorable snags to romance. Maggie May is poor and very proud and the babysitter of surgeon Greg Wilder's three youngest children. Wrapped in their own concerns, neither parent has taken a good long look at the other until one chilly night when Greg comes to pick up his kids . . . and then the magic starts! **DARLING OBSTACLES** is genuinely heartwarming and deeply thrilling. Nine cheers for Barbara Boswell!

(continued)

Passionate and intense, **ENCHANTMENT,** LOVE-SWEPT #96, by Kimberli Wagner is a riveting love story full of sensual tension between two dramatic characters. Alex Kouris and Rhea Morgan are both artists and both mesmerized by one another when they meet. They know immediately that they are kindred souls . . . yet each has a problem to come to terms with before they can realize their destiny together. You won't want to miss Kim's breathtaking romance, which is truly full of **ENCHANTMENT.**

All of us on the LOVESWEPT staff are as fond of Adrienne Staff and Sally Goldenbaum as we are admiring of their skill at creating a unique love story. They make their debut with us in **WHAT'S A NICE GIRL . . . ?,** LOVESWEPT #97. This is the wonderfully humorous and truly touching romance of Susan Rosten and Logan Reed—two people who were meant to find one another across an ocean of differences. Susan comes from a boisterous, warm, close-knit Jewish family; Logan is a rather staid member of the "country club set." Susan owns and operates a local tavern; Logan is a distinguished physician. The resolution of the conflicts between them is often merry, sometimes serious, and always emotionally moving. We believe that after reading **WHAT'S A NICE GIRL . . . ?** you'll be as enthusiastic fans of Adrienne's and Sally's as we are.

And rounding out the month is a superb romance from that superb writer Fayrene Preston. **MISSISSIPPI BLUES,** LOVESWEPT #98, is as witty, as sensually evocative, as emotionally involving as a love story can be! You'll be delighted from the first moments of the provocative (and most unusual) opening of this story until the very last. Fayrene's brash Yankee hero, Kane Benedict, falls for winsome heroine, Suzanna de Francesca, a tenderhearted, passionate woman who has three extraordinary people for whom she's responsible. Suzanna's need to protect her home and its residents clashes violently with Kane's interest in her community. Yet the sultry attraction between them won't—*can't*—be stopped. The charm of Magnolia Trails and the love of Kane and Suzanna will linger with you long after you've finished **MISSISSIPPI BLUES.**

Enjoy!
Sincerely,

Carolyn Nichols

Carolyn Nichols
   Editor
LOVESWEPT
Bantam Books, Inc.
666 Fifth Avenue
New York, NY 10103

Dear Reader:

Meet Belinda Stuart—talented, beautiful, and about to embark on a new life as a successful painter. The only dark place in her heart is occupied by Jack, the tormented husband from whom she has had to separate. Suddenly, just as she's getting her act together, the past comes back to tear her apart.

Back in their carefree days at Harvard, Belinda and her best friend Sally met the men they would marry. Both Jack Stuart and Harry Granger were part of a group who jokingly referred to themselves as "the Ruffians," an irresistibly boisterous club whose loyalty to each other lasted long after their college years. Belinda, captivated by Jack's winning good looks and his talent as a writer, chose him over Harry, but it was Harry who went on to literary fame.

When Harry's hit musical opens in New York, all the Ruffians are there to cheer their friend's success. Two days later tragedy has struck—one of the Ruffians has been murdered, shot point blank in the doorway of Sally and Harry's house. And Belinda is forced to face the fact that the murder is related to her—although she has no idea why.

One by one, every man Belinda has known turns up in the present—Peter Venables, who once loved Belinda and can't believe she doesn't feel the same way for him; Mike Pierce, the perfect gentleman who treats Belinda like a beautiful younger sister; even Harry, Belinda and Jack's most trusted friend—each man with a conflicting story to tell. One is a cold-blooded killer; all prefer to blame Jack than face the horrible truth.

When Belinda and Jack were married, Sally was determined to give them the perfect wedding present, an antique wheel of fortune that would foretell their happy lives together. But now Belinda must return, alone, to the past. She has to uncover the dark secret that has already claimed the life of one person—and may soon claim her own.

Let Dana Clarins thrill you with Belinda's spellbinding story, the unforgettable tale of what happens when a beautiful woman wakes to find herself, alone and frightened, in the middle of her own worst nightmare.

Dana Clarins is a bestselling writer whose books have sold millions of copies under another name. GUILTY PARTIES is the best yet. I'm betting you won't be able to put it down!

Warm regards,

Nessa Rapoport

Nessa Rapoport
Senior Editor

S ALLY CAME OFF THE ELEVATOR carrying in her arms, like a gigantic infant, a cascade of yellow roses wrapped in tissue, tied loosely with a thick yellow ribbon, a floppy bow. She marched on into the kitchen and began searching for vases.

"What in the world—" I said.

"You've got paint all over your face, dear. Two vases aren't going to be enough." She was wearing a pale blue linen dress, sleeveless, with white piping. She was too pale herself for the outfit but with the jet-black hair and the sharp angles of her face she looked great.

I found her a third vase. "What is this?"

"For you. They were propped on that pathetic little wooden chair down in the lobby. Just sitting there. I asked a man carrying a box bigger than East Rutherford into the warehouse if he'd seen them delivered. He told me he couldn't see where he was going, let alone check out deliverymen. Here's a card."

I tore open the envelope.

Apologies are in order. I'll make them in person.

The fan on the counter passed its waves across my face like the flutter of invisible wings, and I felt a shiver ripple along my spine. Sally was watching me, hands on hips, feet apart, waiting impatiently. "So what does it say?"

I handed it to her and she cocked her head inquisitively. The light at the windows was reflecting the deep purple of the afternoon sky. The first raindrops were tapping on the skylight. I couldn't tell her about Venables. I'd told him I wouldn't and he was their houseguest on top of that and the show was opening and who needed any more problems?

And Sal and I didn't tell each other everything, anyway. Not anymore.

"May I ask what that is supposed to mean?"

I made a face. "It's nothing. A guy . . . a guy I barely know made a mistake the other night . . ." I shrugged.

"Ah, the adventures of the newly single!" She picked up two of the vases and smiled at me quizzically. "Well,

I won't pry. But let it be recorded that I am utterly fascinated."

"It's not very fascinating. Let that be recorded."

I followed her into the work area. The thunder's first crack went off like a cannon and I flinched. Like a child frightened by loud noises and the gathering darkness.

"I'm betting on Jack. Or—hmmm—could it be Mike?"

"What? What are you talking about?"

"Belinda, are you all right?"

"Yes, of course, I'm fine."

"The flowers. I was talking about the flowers—I'll bet they're from Jack, who misbehaved and is sorry . . . or from Mike. I mean, you have been seeing Mike—"

"Please, Sal. Mike is an old friend. You know that—we've had dinner a couple of times and Mike is the spitting image of Bertie Wooster and he's a dear. But he never, never would make a mistake about me. Okay? I rest my case."

Sally was leaning against the wheel-of-fortune, staring out into the rain, nodding. I mopped sweat from my face and dropped the towel on the table.

"All right, all right. It's your secret." She pressed a forefinger to her lips, looking at me from the corners of her eyes. . . .

The afternoon wore on. The loft darkened. Lightning continued to crackle over the city like electrical stems, jagged, plunging down into the heart of Manhattan. The rain came down like dishwater emptying out of a sink. Sally had another drink and sucked on the bright green wedge of lime. The yellow roses glowed as if they were lit from within. I listened to Sally talk about men, the show, Harry and Jack. . . .

One moment she was laughing and then the thunder hammered at the skylight again and her face began to come apart and redefine itself as if she were about to burst into tears.

"Are you all right, Sal?" I went to her, wanting to help.
She turned quickly away, back to the wheel-of-fortune.

"Let's see what the gods hold for tonight, a hit or a miss." She sniffled, spun the wheel, planted her feet apart as if challenging the future. It finally clicked to a halt.

Sal read it slowly. "'You will have everything you have hoped for.'"

She looked at me, trying to smile.

"Oh," she said, "everything is such a mess, honey." She began to cry with her head on my shoulder. I put my arm around her, felt the shuddering as Sally clung to me. I cooed to her. Everything would be all right. But as I stroked her shiny black hair, the paintings in the shadows caught my eye and I wasn't sure.

* * *

AT SIX O'CLOCK THE CROWD clogged the street in front of the theater, the lucky ones squeezed beneath the marquee with its *Scoundrels All!* logo in Harvard crimson. Everyone was dressed up and soaked through with perspiration and sprays of rain. Everyone seemed to be shouting to be heard, faces were red, laughter too loud. Bright, artificial smiles looked like the direct result of root-canal work. Hope was everywhere. The sight made me wonder if my own opening would be so frantic, so harried, so riddled with fear and tension.

I held onto Mike's arm, smiled faintly at familiar faces, and nodded at snatches of conversation I couldn't quite make out. The whole scene was a kind of orgy of self-consciousness, people with a good deal to lose but trying not to show it, pretending that nothing hung in the balance. Another opening, another show.

Harry's head was visible above the crowd, inclined to the comments of two men I recognized by sight, one a legendary womanizer and show-business angel, the other a famous agent who knew everyone and never missed anything. At a party once years before I'd seen him take a package of chewing gum from the beringed hand of a very young woman with turquoise and purple hair and Jack had whispered to me: "See that? That's how they do it. Cocaine wrapped in five little sticks, like gum." He'd been terribly amused when at first I couldn't believe it.

A large, bulky man in a very crumpled linen jacket with a floppy silk handkerchief dribbling from the pocket looked benignly out across the crowd from Harry's side. He alone seemed serene and somewhat amused by the proceedings, as if his cumbersome size kept him from becoming too frantic. I'd seen him before, I was sure of it, but where? I was watching him without really being aware of it when he caught my eye, seemed to be staring at me, expressionless. Then, as if he'd made a connection that was just eluding me, he slowly grinned and I looked away. Should I have known him? He wasn't the type you'd forget.

Mike was waving at people, chattering away. The show's director stood more or less alone, a tiny bearded man, looking like a child's toy wound right to the breaking point. He glanced at his watch, then disappeared through the stage door. Slowly the crowd began to push through the doors, through the lobby, down the red-carpeted aisles toward their seats. The black uniformed ushers whisked up and down, checking tickets, handing out programs.

My stomach was knotted, my throat dry, and I wondered how Sally was holding up. I couldn't see her in the crowd. Mike Nichols was a few rows ahead of us, standing, still wearing a rain-spotted, belted trench coat, his face amazingly boyish beneath the blondish hair. There was Tony LoBianco, dark and handsome, radiating energy and intensity, as if he were about to spring at someone or something. Doc Simon, shy and tall and scholarly, was talking to a man who looked like a banker, which figured, since the playwright had finally, officially, made all the money in the known universe.

Scanning the faces, I knew I was actually looking for the two I hoped most weren't there. Jack. And Peter Venables. The thought of both men was pushing my stomach off center. Praying I wouldn't turn and come face to face with them, praying for the easy way out. I kept thinking of Jack slamming the phone down and cutting Sally off . . . and Peter's beautiful yellow roses and the note that filled me with dread. *Apologies are in order. I'll make them in person.*

Finally, thank God, the houselights dimmed and I hadn't seen either of them.

Within seconds I felt as if the curtain had gone up on a kind of personal psychodrama, as if I'd stumbled straight off the edge of the real world and was free-falling through time.

* * *

FOR SOME REASON THAT SUMMER nobody had quite bothered to prepare me for the show I saw. Maybe it was because I had been so wrapped up in my own work, maybe because I hadn't been listening when they tried. Whatever the reason, I wasn't in the least prepared once the actors and actresses had taken the stage, and it was hard to shake free of the disorientation.

With music and dancing and a witty book, *Scoundrels All!* was *our* story, the story of the Ruffians and Sally and me, and it came at me in a series of waves, reviving memories I'd never known were buried in my subconscious, memories of people and events I hadn't been aware of at the time. It was like seeing one of Alex Katz's paintings in a Fifty-seventh Street gallery, a scene of his sharp-featured people at a cocktail party, pretty women with flat, predatory looks, well-dressed men with cuffs showing just the right amount as they climbed one social or business ladder after another . . . like seeing the paintings and slowly realizing that you were there, you'd been one of the people at the party. It was both unnerving and seductive and I felt myself almost guiltily being excited by what I saw, as if it were my own private secret.

I'd been so wrapped up in my own concerns in those days that I'd hardly noticed the world around me. Classes, clothes, time spent with Sally, driving her little red convertible along narrow leaf-blown roads, working in the studio at all hours, painting and losing track of time, then meeting Harry Granger . . . and later Jack Stuart.

Now, astonished, I watched all our lives cavorting across the stage, laughter rippling and applause exploding from the audience. Reality had been softened and given pastel hues at it was filtered through the lens of nostalgia. Like a faint recollection that had almost slipped through the cracks of memory, my past was coming back to life, and we were all up there on the stage. Whatever names they were called, they were us. Jack, the athlete with the handsome face, tossing a football in the air, singing a song about the big game Saturday with Yale . . . Mike wearing white duck slacks and a straw boater at a jaunty angle, dancing an engaging soft-shoe . . . Harry politicking his friends about his idea for a club, an oath of loyalty, and a commitment for a lifetime, all so innocent and idealistic . . . and there were the girls, a blond and a brunette arriving on the stage in a snazzy red convertible.

I was having some difficulty keeping the lines between fact and fiction from blurring. Which was the real Belinda? The one on stage or the nearly middle-aged one watching? Did I really say that? Is that the way I behaved, the way I appeared to others—the self-centered ultra-Wasp who seemed to pluck for herself first one man and then the other?

The love stories wound sinuously, sometimes comically, through the saga of the founding of the club and the conflicts among the members and the crisis of the football game . . . Harry falling in love with the blond, then losing her to Jack, then Harry taking sudden notice of the brunette.

But it was all in a kind of fairyland where the hurts never lasted and everybody finally loved everyone else and everything was all right. . . . Jack was singing alone in a spotlight, wearing a corny letter sweater with the flickering illusion of a pep-rally bonfire through a scrim behind him. Not much like Harvard, really, it might have been an

rtifact like the Thurber and Nugent play, *The Male
Animal*, it all seemed so quaint and long ago. Jack was
singing about the blond girl he'd fallen for and how he was
going to have to take her away from his best pal Harry and
would it wreck their friendship and how could one Scoun-
drel do such a thing to another?

And, like a sentimental fool, I thanked God for the
darkness of the theater. My cheek was wet with tears.

A Stirring Novel of Destinies
Bound by Unquenchable Passion

SUNSET EMBRACE

by Sandra Brown

Fate threw Lydia Russell and Ross Coleman, two untame
outcasts, together on a Texas-bound wagon train. On that wil
road, they fought the breathtaking desire blazing between them
while the shadows of their enemies grew longer. As the trai
rolled west, danger drew ever closer, until a showdown wit
their pursuers was inevitable. Before it was over, Lydia an
Ross would face death . . . the truth about each other . . . an
the astonishing strength of·their love.

Buy SUNSET EMBRACE, on sale January 15, 198
wherever Bantam paperbacks are sold, or use the handy cou
pon below for ordering:

**A stunning novel of romance
and intrigue by**

THE
FOREVER DREAM
by Iris Johansen

...ania Orlinov is prima ballerina for a New York ...llet company. Jared Ryker is a brilliant scientist ...hose genetics research has brought him to the ...rink of discovering how to extend human life for ...o to 500 years. A chance meeting brings them ...gether—and now nothing can keep them apart.

...HE FOREVER DREAM has all the passion, extraor-...narily sensual lovemaking and romance that have ...come Iris Johansen's signature, plus the tension ...nd suspense of a first-rate thriller. In her longest ...nd most far-reaching novel to date, Iris Johansen ...ps all our fantasies of romantic love and explores ...he fascinating implications of practical immortality.

...on't miss THE FOREVER DREAM, available wher-...ver Bantam Books are sold, or use this handy cou-...on for ordering:

#1 HEAVEN'S PRICE
By Sandra Brown
Blair Simpson had enclosed herself in the fortress of her dancing, but Sean Garrett was determined to love her anyway. In his arms she came to understand the emotions behind her dancing. But could she afford the high price of love?

#2 SURRENDER
By Helen Mittermeyer
Derry had been pirated from the church by her ex-husband, from under the nose of the man she was to marry. She remembered every detail that had driven them apart—and the passion that had drawn her to him. The unresolved problems between them grew . . . but their desire swept them toward surrender.

#3 THE JOINING STONE
By Noelle Berry McCue
Anger and desire warred within her, but Tara Burns was determined not to let Damon Mallory know her feelings. When he'd walked out of their marriage, she'd been hurt.

Damon had violated a sacred trust, yet her passion for him was as breathtaking as the Grand Canyon.

#4 SILVER MIRACLES
By Fayrene Preston
Silver-haired Chase Colfax stood in the Texas moonlight, then took Trinity Ann Warrenton into his arms. Overcome by her own needs, yet determined to have him on her own terms, she struggled to keep from losing herself in his passion.

#5 MATCHING WITS
By Carla Neggers
From the moment they met, Ryan Davis tried to outmaneuver Abigail Lawrence. She'd met her match in the Back Bay businessman. And Ryan knew the Boston lawyer was more woman than any he'd ever encountered. Only if they vanquished their need to best the other could their love triumph.

#6 A LOVE FOR ALL TIME
By Dorothy Garlock
A car crash had left its marks on Casey Farrow's beauty. So what were Dan

Murdock's motives for pursuing her? Guilt? Pity? Casey had to choose. She could live with doubt and fear . . . or learn a lesson in love.

Michael Brady from the moment he brought the breezes of life into her shadowy existence. Yet a specter of the past remained to torment her and threaten their future. Could he subdue the demons that haunted her, and carry her to true happiness?

#12 HUNTER'S PAYNE
By Joan J. Domning
P. Lee Payne strode into Karen Hunter's office demanding to know why she was stalking him. She was determined to interview the mysterious photographer. She uncovered his concealed emotions, but could the secrets their hearts confided protect their love, or would harsh daylight shatter their fragile alliance?

#13 TIGER LADY
By Joan J. Domning
Who *was* this mysterious lover she'd never seen who courted her on the office computer, and nicknamed her Tiger Lady? And could he compete with Larry Hart, who came to repair the computer and stayed to short-cir-

cuit her emotions? How could she choose between poetry and passion—between soul and Hart?

#14 STORMY VOWS
By Iris Johansen
Independent Brenna Sloan wasn't strong enough to reach out for the love she needed, and Michael Donovan knew only how to take—until he met Brenna. Only after a misunderstanding nearly destroyed their happiness, did they surrender to their fiery passion.

#15 BRIEF DELIGHT
By Helen Mittermeyer
Darius Chadwick felt his chest tighten with desire as Cygnet Melton glided into his life. But a prelude was all they knew before Cyg fled in despair, certain she had shattered the dream they had made together. Their hearts had collided in an instant; now could they seize the joy of enduring love?

#16 A VERY RELUCTANT KNIGHT
By Billie Green
A tornado brought them together in a storm cel-

lar. But Maggie Sims and Mark Wilding were anything but perfectly matched. Maggie wanted to prove he was wrong about her. She knew they didn't belong together, but when he caressed her, she was swept up in a passion that promised a lifetime of love.

#17 TEMPEST AT SEA
By Iris Johansen
Jane Smith sneaked aboard playboy-director Jake Dominic's yacht on a dare. The muscled arms that captured her were inescapable—and suddenly Jane found herself agreeing to a month-long cruise of the Caribbean. Jane had never given much thought to love, but under Jake's tutelage she discovered its magic . . . and its torment.

#18 AUTUMN FLAMES
By Sara Orwig
Lily Dunbar had ventured too far into the wilderness of Reece Wakefield's vast Chilean ranch; now an oncoming storm thrust her into his arms . . . and he refused to let her go. Could he lure her, step by seductive step, away from the life she had forged for herself, to find her real home in his arms?

#19 PFARR LAKE AFFAIR
By Joan J. Domning
Leslie Pfarr hadn't been back at her father's resort for an hour before she was pitched into the lake by Eric Nordstrom! The brash teenager who'd made her childhood a constant torment had grown into a handsome man. But when he began persuading her to fall in love, Leslie wondered if she was courting disaster.

#20 HEART ON A STRING
By Carla Neggers
One look at heart surgeon Paul Houghton Welling told JoAnna Radcliff he belonged in the stuffy society world she'd escaped for a cottage in Pigeon Cove. She firmly believed she'd never fit into his life, but he set out to show her she was wrong. She was the puppet master, but he knew how to keep her heart on a string.

#21 THE SEDUCTION OF JASON
By Fayrene Preston
On vacation in Martinique, Morgan Saunders found Jason Falco. When a misunderstanding drove him away, she had to win him back. She played the seductress to tempt him to return; she sent him tropical flowers to tantalize him; she wrote her love in letters twenty feet high—on a billboard that echoed the words in her heart.

#22 BREAKFAST IN BED
By Sandra Brown
For all Sloan Fairchild knew, Hollywood had moved to San Francisco when mystery writer Carter Madison stepped into her bed-and-breakfast inn. In his arms the forbidden longing that throbbed between them erupted. Sloan had to choose—between her love for him and her loyalty to a friend . . .

#23 TAKING SAVANNAH
By Becky Combs
The Mercedes was headed straight for her! Cassie hurled a rock that smashed the antique car's taillight. The price driver Jake Kilrain exacted was a passionate kiss, and he set out to woo the Southern lady, Cassie, but discovered that his efforts to conquer the lady might end in his own surrender . . .

#24 THE RELUCTANT LARK
By Iris Johansen
Her haunting voice had earned Sheena Reardon fame as Ireland's mournful dove. Yet to Rand Challon the young singer was not just a lark but a woman whom he desired with all his heart. Rand knew he could teach her to spread her wings and fly free, but would her flight take her from him or into his arms forever?